I0713693

R. Wesley Clement

Rogue Wave

Rogue Wave
Copyright © 2023 by R. Wesley Clement

All rights reserved. No part of this publication may be
reproduced, distributed, or transmitted in any form or
by any means, including photocopying, recording, or
other electronic or mechanical methods, without the prior
written permission of the author, except in the case of
brief quotations embodied in critical reviews and certain
other non-commercial uses permitted by copyright law.

ISBN
978-1-961250-91-8 (Paperback)
978-1-961250-92-5 (eBook)
978-1-961250-90-1 (Hardcover)

Rogue Wave

TABLE OF CONTENTS

The stairs groan with each step, the railing squeaks as hands find purchase. Like Zombies, three sisters in turn pause to look into the middle distance before moving heavily downward. One after another they descend as if about to enter a coal mine.

The youngest, Dorothy, the last to take her turn in the bathroom and the last on the stairs joins her sisters in the kitchen.

Armed with a bowl of cereal she drags a third chair away from the table and sits down with a thump. No smiles reach out to welcome their youngest sister to the table.

Three sisters lost in the mouth of their cereal bowls, eyes buried deep; chewing sounds the only conversation.

Unconsciously and in tandem their eyes leave their bowls and turn to their parent's bedroom. Deep sighs follow. No voice suggests what today might bring.

Then with the tick of a clock the girls have rinsed and placed their bowls in the sink grabbed their back packs and scurried out the door and onto a bus that waits for no man.

The grim face of the driver wears his own frozen expression of resignation. In the mirror he watches the girls jockey for a seat, their eyes cast downward mouths drawn in a straight line.

With the folding door closed and the girls seated, a curl of exhaust signals movement; vapor dissipating like a ghost losing its mojo.

The street, absent of kids going off to war, quiets.

The Garrett house seemingly shudders from a cold wind coming off the water several streets away.

Within the house all remains quiet until the heat comes on, a ticking sound announcing its arrival to each room.

As the heat makes its rounds the heated air releases recent smells of this morning's showers mixed with a lingering smell of earlier brewed coffee.

An hour before the girls made their way to the kitchen, Wayne Garrett, the man of the house, had limped to the sideboard and managed to brew, pour and balance two cups of Joe all the while navigating crutches.

Now back in the master bedroom, he and wife Becky nurse their coffee whispering their own concerns of what new shoe might drop today.

When the girls made their way down stairs earlier, what should have been a morning filled with lively banter and kidding, was instead a wall of silence.

These days the girls' father doesn't witness his daughters going about their morning routine. He sighs. For all that is going on it's just as well. Wayne blames himself for what the family is going through.

In the not so distant past before leaving for work he greeted each daughter as they descended the stairs with humor, mussed their hair, told a recent post office joke or sung one of his, (to his daughters' minds) stupid songs.

In this present day house of gloom, silence serves as a constant companion to all activity.

The bedroom door opens and Wayne Garrett awkwardly makes his way back to the kitchen. Wife Becky wounded in a different way shuffles slowly behind, her eyes too cast downward. After reaching opposite ends of the kitchen table their eyes vacant of hope slowly rise to acknowledge one another. With mouths hanging slack like melted wax, long mournful sighs break the silence.

The world is awake though. A rising, stretching, yawning, morning sun rides a brisk wind bringing light to the gloom. Wayne's face, illuminated by a stray sunbeam, reveals a graying grizzled visage not seen by a razor in a long while.

Becky, sitting opposite face still in shadow, watches her husband attempt to brew a second pot of coffee.

She offers to help.

In a barely audible voice Wayne refuses. With his back turned and his crutches leaning against the counter he grabs the counter-top for support and watches the amber liquid slowly enter the pot, lost in thought.

Becky hasn't moved from her seat. She mindlessly turns the pages of the morning paper not a single word registering. She barely raises her eyes as a second cup arrives; merely nodding her head in thanks. Raising her cup in tandem with the morning headlines the paper hides her face. Coffee at both ends of the table emptied in silence.

* * *

The bus drops the girls off like dominoes, from youngest to oldest, shortest to tallest. Elementary School for Dorothy, Middle School for Shellee, and now the last domino stands watching the bus head back to wherever.

The oldest, Marla, lingers before entering the High school. As she looks out over the student parking lot a thought reaches her mind. *A time not that long ago she would have parked her first car, gathered her books, excited,as she hurried to enter the school for her senior year.*

Three sisters seated in three different schools at three different desks in three different classrooms share one common thought that will consume their day. ***When will this nightmare end!***

CHAPTER ONE

Six months ago

Wayne Garrett works for the post office. He delivers mail to the residents in the city of Flagler Beach, Florida. His route includes a nearly five-mile business district that is defined by route A1A and across that ribbon of black top; the Atlantic Ocean. This small coastal city of eight thousand like nearly every other small city has a main thoroughfare. Unlike most however, where sovereignty ends with a road sign, Flagler Beach marks the end of its eastern geography at the shores of the mighty Atlantic Ocean.

Route 100, an east to west four lane highway, that splits the town in two geographically, feeds into the city from the west. Blue water and cresting waves appear just as you begin descending a long steep overpass that spans an Inter-coastal waterway.

At the eastern end of this long span a traffic light offers the first of two warnings; water just ahead.

If you choose to continue in a straight line for an eighth of a mile there is still one more chance, one more opportunity to turn left for north or right to travel south on Route A1A and avoid a day at the beach. Going straight through that final light will drown all your aspirations.

For geographical purposes, three and a half miles to the south on Route A1A with the Atlantic Ocean on your left, a sign for Volusia County appears. A dozen miles south Ormond Beach, grabs your attention followed by Daytona Beach; Volusia county's most famous resident.

Choosing to travel north at the final stoplight a left turn allows a view of the mighty Atlantic on your right for nearly a dozen miles where you enter St. John's County. Adozen more miles will deliver you to the Bridge of Lions in the heart of the oldest city in America, St Augustine.

Sandwiched between the two well-known cities St. Augustine and Daytona Beach, the small city of Flagler Beach offers its own uniqueness. Flagler Beach dances to the beat of a different drummer.

You would be hard pressed to find chain restaurants or franchised businesses along A1A in Flagler County, Florida. Rather an eclectic and diverse number of establishments; restaurants, small motels, bars, souvenir and beach wear, bike and surfboard rentals, and Ice cream shops; all chase the tourist dollar.

Just across A1A the Atlantic Ocean provides its own form of entertainment. Beach walking, surf fishing, sun bathing, picnicking, or splashing in the waves dominate the activity. Away from the shore surf boards dot the water. A mile out from there shrimp boats line the horizon reminding us that tourist dollar be damned, most people have to work for a living.

Back across the highway a lone high rise, the <u>Aliki</u>, stands looking out over the town and the Atlantic Ocean. That single building of a dozen stories serves as a reminder to the city fathers that to their mind all progress is not necessarily forward thinking.

Old timers still lament what they were talked into. But the past is the past and most residents simply use this twelve-story outlier as a marker for where they are in relation to where they are going.

* * *

Wayne Garrett and his family live on the south side of the city three blocks back from the ocean, Ninth Street S.

The Garrett home has been around much longer than its fifty-year- old owner. The house was one of the nicest houses in town back in the day. It is still well kept and boasts a second story overlooking a well-manicured oversized lot complete with a garden patch. Wayne Garrett received the house from a man who had previously owned the home and a four-floor tenement building.

Years ago Jamie Collins the previous owner grew up in the house, and took over the property and a tenement building, chose not to live in the house but occupied an apartment on the first floor of the tenement building. Jamie Collins rented the fourth floor to Wayne and his parents when Wayne was just a boy.

When Jamie Collins returned home from a career in the military, he chose not to occupy his beautiful home. The house was rented out to some friends of his family and Jamie allowed them to stay. The four apartments in the tenement building were also rented so Jamie took an apartment near the water.

Later when forced to deal with some issues in one of his rents he chose to occupy the first floor of his tenement building.

It was on the porch of that building that young Wayne Garrett learned many life lessons from Jamie Collins. Sitting side by side in matching rocking chairs life lessons emerged through folklore voiced in an Irish tragedy sort of way.

Using long convoluted Irish lore to explain events, Wayne, just a kid, listened and at first simply nodded in all the right places.

Wayne carried the lessons learned and acted on them for most of the time he has been on this earth. The lasting bond with his benefactor was unshakeable.

This morning, such a beautiful morning filled with promises made, Wayne made his way to the Post Office

Wayne does not realize this beautiful morning is about to change in a storm of events that will impact the lives of the entire Garrett family for the foreseeable future.

* * *

As this morning begins Wayne Garrett at age fifty is a happy man, resilient, forward thinking; ask anyone.

He happily mows his own lawn, constantly humming just loud enough to cover the sound of the mower in his ears. He also trims his own shrubs and trees while whistling aloud and off tune. Wayne is one of the few residents who maintains their own property. No commercial mowers and landscapers for him. Happily going about his business, he has often been stopped by passers-by inquiring whether he might consider maintaining their property.

Mistaken for a landscaper the conversation usually goes like this: A man gets out and asks if Wayne does lawns. Wayne smiles to himself the joke already taking shape in his head. He answers, "Yes I do."

'Well, what do you charge?'

The smile broadens as Wayne responds, "Actually I have a good gig going with the lady of the house."

'How do you mean?'

"Well, the lady of the house cooks for me for one thing."

'Really.'

"Yep." Then drawing things out a little longer with an even wider smile Wayne adds, "I even get to sleep with the lady occasionally!"

When a look of shock and dismay crosses the man's face, Wayne finally holds up his hands in defense with a genuine grin on his face. "I actually live here. I am the owner." Wayne has repeated that story at the post office a dozen times over the years, always prompting a good laugh.

As I said, Wayne is a happy man. He enjoys walks along the ocean with his wife and occasionally his girls. They are growing up fast and more often than not, lately prefer to do their own thing.

Over the years Wayne has made an occasional feeble attempt to surf, but was never really good at it. He was always too busy with a paper route that took on a life of its own. These days he rides a bike with his wife and those same reluctant daughters tag along like a line of ducks biking the side streets across from the ocean.

When he can corral his daughters to join them on those rides, Wayne leaves the girls shaking their heads at his antics.

Wayne brings up the rear on these twice a week adventures, like a mother duck, always with one eye seeking someone to wave to, shout out to, or stop and chat with; all the while keeping his other eye open to protect his loved ones from harm.

So, it could safely be said Wayne Garrett has lived his life a happy man. **That is until today!**

Lyrics from that Garth Brooks song, *If I'd only known, how the king would fall, who knows I might have missed it all,* hadn't reached the ears of Wayne Garrett on this early summer morning. Wayne, if he'd known what today was going to foist upon the backs of his entire family would have been glad to miss, *The Dance.*

* * *

But let's just start with the sorting of the mail. Wayne waves as his fellow employees arrive to fill their own deliveries. He has a kind word for each of them. He spends the first hour of his workday sorting the mail and loading up the plastic tubs that line his jeep-like vehicle.

Whistling just below the surface he is trying to place a song he'd heard the tail end of driving in to work this morning.

Wayne loves his job and takes it seriously. To Wayne the mail is sacred. Putting personal importance to his efforts he truly believes any given piece of mail can be a life changer for the recipient.

Even still, sorting mail is kinda mundane. Wayne can do the sorting while thinking of other things and so his mind wanders. Wayne thinks of his three girls who started back to school a week ago dressed in very different outfits suggesting very different personalities but the three girls are a source of constant happiness for their parents

A drop of sweat reaches his nose. Still hot as Hades in the Sunshine State of Florida, this last week of August. Wayne's thoughts move to include the smell of barbecued chicken being served tonight. Wayne's eyes water at the memory of the pungent onions he peeled for wife Becky, as she put together a potato salad yesterday afternoon. Wayne had been charged with picking fresh tomatoes and cukes from the little garden in the back that he tends religiously.

Wayne sighs even as his hands with a mind of their own put the mail in its proper order.

Just the two of them on the patio toasting their lives with a cold beer before dinner reaches his mind. Even firing up the grill and swallowing smoke can't remove the smile from his face.

Another and even more pleasant thought for later, after the girls are in bed, brings a shy inner smile. When you get to a certain age things seem to take place with more deliberation than sudden emotion. Tonight is an agreed upon night, so Wayne doesn't have to think about getting lucky tonight. It is marked on his internal calendar. He begins to hum a bit louder.

When the mail is sorted and the tubs placed in the Jeep in a fashion that supports an ordered delivery, Wayne checks his mirrors then starts the Jeep.

He leaves the post office loading area as other mail carriers are leaving for their own canvass of the town. Wayne's head is clear, evening plans as in place as his bins of mail.

He doesn't notice the extra-long withering look that follows him from the edge of the post office parking lot. He doesn't see the Jeep that sits idling on the side of the road.

He is still humming that tune he heard this morning but can't put a name to. He reaches and enters A1A heading north. Some of his route will have him delivering from the truck and at other times loading up his well-worn leather carrier to deliver on foot.

He passes a number of businesses that crowd the first half mile of A1A north. He remembers delivering newspapers on foot nearly forty years ago to some of these same addresses.

He glances at the Golden Lion, one of the family's favorite restaurants, quiet now but give it a few hours and the roof top tables will be filled with locals and visitors.

The single high rise, the Aliki, looms in the near distance. He delivers mail to that building first. He empties a whole tub of mail, magazines, and fliers into row after row of mail slots that he feeds from the back. As he places today's mail his mind wanders once again. The sounds of the Atlantic lulls him into another daydream.

The girls are at school he won't see them until tonight. This past summer though with the girls out of school he had allowed himself to linger, nursing a second cup of coffee till he heard them stir and come down with their hair all askew. Even in his reverie he smiles. *Feeling each of them returning more reluctant hugs as they mature, youngest daughter Dorothy the last to fully embrace her father in an unrestrained manner. His marching orders for their day are greeted with less than enthusiasm, but are eventually followed.* Still everything about summer was a little more relaxing.

The snow birds had long been gone and the level of mail and his workload dwindled in the searing heat.

Back in his Jeep shaking himself back to the present, he has to brake to avoid a wild turkey who had somehow made it to the beach. Shortly he is daydreaming once more. *Summer vacation is over, a new school year is upon them, my god Marla is a senior.* His mind turns to his wife who has the luxury of lingering a little longer in the bed they share, she is always awake though. In his mind Wayne can see her there with a smile on her lips listening in as their father gives the girls their marching orders for the day.

In the summer those orders included house work, gardening chores, and admonishments to be wary of the rip currents when they venture to the beach.

This morning though with the first day of the second week of school underway the only sounds had come from the girls themselves, giggling and teasing, sisters being sisters. The oldest, Marla, just last evening began negotiating for her first car. Wayne was even now contemplating what that might mean.

*   *   *

With the slam of the door and the sound of the squeak of the arriving bus, the house quieted. Becky Garrett will rise to nurse a second cup of coffee before showering then heading to the souvenir shop she manages on A1A. She played out the best part of her day in her head.

Wayne will be meeting her for his break at nine thirty, a routine that daily has them looking into one another's eyes, savoring the good life they are living. Now with school starting and Wayne leaving for work earlier, the little doughnut shop sitting adjacent to the souvenir shop provides the couple with a quiet moment. Seated at a small table across A1A from the mighty Atlantic Ocean, often a fishing boat appears on the horizon changing the conversation from family matters to speculation about what it would be like out there on the open sea. With the evening menu set and Wayne shyly raising his eyes and suggesting the evenings' (after hours dessert). A clinking of mugs and knowing smiles signals time to get back to work for both.

*   *   *

Wayne, slim and fit for fifty walks three miles of his ten-mile route daily, parking his Jeep at points along the way and filling his mail bag for a crisscrossing of side streets.

Getting out of the Jeep allows him to stretch his legs and his mind to wander. Loaded up, Wayne takes a moment to study his face in the side mirror before nodding to himself; satisfied. His daily walk, evening strolls, and biking with his family at night has helped keep a double chin from taking up residence. The dreaded beer gut he sees on so many men his age threatening to give birth has not appeared.

Wife Becky too remains committed to her own wellness. *Yes*, he thinks as he returns to his jeep for a reload, *I am a lucky guy*.

He takes a deep breath. With a second carrier of mail delivered he re-enters the Jeep sits for a moment and turns the ignition; nothing. Not even a grind from the starter. Wayne takes a second deep breath.

Studying his eyes in the rear-view mirror as if willing a better result, he nods to himself and once more turns the key. Once again; no, nothing, nada. His deep breath turns into a sigh.

Wayne is many things but a mechanic he is not. He calls in to the office on his cell. It might be an hour or more before anyone can assist him he is told. *Wonderful! Will I make it to have coffee with Becky?* He checks his watch; *a maybe at best*.

He doesn't wait for his supervisor to tell him what he's already figured out for himself before hanging up. He gets out of the jeep and refills his battered carrier to begin what promises to be a longer than normal delivery day.

Before beginning his walk he checks his watch once more and calls his wife Becky who is still at home and tells her he probably in all likelihood won't be having coffee with her this morning.

He doesn't explain the problem. "I'll see you at home. Looks like it will be a good evening for a bike ride; after the barbecue of course, and before our **scheduled appointment**."

"What appointment is that Wayne, we got an insurance guy coming to the house you didn't tell me about?"

Wayne has to chuckle, "Funny you."

"Well I hope the rest of your day goes better dear, see you tonight. Hope your night goes better too, those Insurance guys can keep you for hours," Becky was laughing out loud now.

Exasperated by his wife's humor, Wayne signs off with a simple, "Bye now."

Wayne puts his whistle back in place while still trying to identify that damn song; Garth Brooks maybe? He begins delivering to mailboxes that normally only see his arm exit his vehicle.

A woman leaving her house waves and smiles."So that's what you look like."

Wayne is still in a good mood. "Yeah I'm more than just a pretty arm," he kids.

The woman catches the humor and laughs aloud.

Wayne continues delivering magazines, circulars, and regular mail along Eighth Street in a westerly direction which will eventually take him all the way to the Inter-Coastal. But not today; not yet at least. He is out of mail. He'll have to return to the Jeep and reload. He checks his watch. A half hour has gone by.

He thinks of his wife at work now and soon to be at the little table having coffee. Wayne sighs aloud. For some reason his wife's attempt at humor earlier reaches his mind. They share a love for a long running theme from the television hit <u>Seinfeld</u>, *NO SOUP FOR YOU!* He chuckles, still in a good frame of mind.

What appears to be a mail vehicle appears and pulls up beside him. A hat shades a face that nods, no words are exchanged as the driver drives off. Wayne doesn't recognize the vehicle or the driver but that doesn't mean much, a lot of the rural carriers drive their own personal vehicles and someone new was always being hired.

Wayne thinks that the guy just driving off like that a little odd but doesn't dwell on it.

During the walk back Wayne is musing. He checks his watch again. *If this guy is any kind of a mechanic he might just catch the rear end of coffee and conversation with his wife after all. He will make clear there will be no insurance guy joining them in their bedroom tonight.* He laughs aloud and begins whistling again watching his feet hit the pavement. Still the name of the song in his head eludes him, though the lyrics are beginning to take shape. A bounce returns to his step. When he eventually arrives back to his own Jeep the other Jeep has apparently come and gone. *Must have been an easy fix,* thinks Wayne. He smiles, already tasting that mug of coffee.

Wayne returns his leather carrier to the vehicle while he begins a trip through his mental Rolodex. *Who was that guy? If my Jeep is fixed I'll have to thank him.*

Wayne turns the key and the vehicle roars to life. *Yes!*

The speed limits on these side streets in this little beach town are slow by design. What with work vans parked outside many houses on any given day, Stop signs at nearly every side street, and a local law that allows golf carts as a source of transportation; slow is the operative word.

Wayne puts his Jeep into drive and touches the gas pedal. He edges slowly back onto the roadway, his mind on that fresh cup of coffee drowning what was beginning to shape up as a bad hair day. He looks ahead then his eyes check the rear-view.

Turning his eyes back to the front he touches the gas catching a glimpse of another damn wild turkey crossing in front of him.

The engine suddenly accelerates. He yanks the wheel to the right and slams his brakes. The vehicle doesn't slow and barely misses the turkey. The engine continues to roar. The Jeep lurches across the roadway as if starving for attention. In a nanosecond he has crossed the street and is climbing a steep lawn and entering a living room window at 38 Eighth Street N. Glass shatters as the window casings splinter showering the front of the Jeep.

His vehicle plows through a coffee table and a couch, then like one of those toy monster trucks tries to climb an inner wall, the engine continuing to roar.

In the process of getting from here to there Wayne bangs his head pretty good, mangles some limbs, but doesn't pass out; not immediately anyway.

Sitting there dazed and damaged still strapped in, his heart racing, the engine roaring, blood beginning to enter his eyes, he thinks it is a white cloud he's seeing, in reality it's a ceiling.

Wayne is confused and beginning to enter shock. His right arm won't assist him in turning off the ignition, it hangs useless.

Fading fast he manages with his left hand to shut off the noise. Pain suddenly engulfs him as the first phase of shock really kicks in. Blood continues to enter his eyes from a head wound and a mask of darkness descends upon him.

His consciousness stirs, pain returns. *How did I get here?* His first thought. He doesn't see but rather feels the driver's side door open. Before he goes completely blank once again he manages to open one eye. He would later swear someone was standing there pointing at him, laughing, and then the movie faded back to black.

The police and ambulance arrive and Wayne is loaded for transport to Flagler Hospital. On the way Wayne begins to re-emerge from the blackness once again.

A trauma team is waiting and Wayne is removed to a dolly that moves rapidly into the bowels of the emergency room. All kinds of shouting accompanies him on his trip. Orders are barked which adds to Wayne's confusion.

In his mind a highlight reel of odd bits of data is playing out. *(Odd man showing up to fix his Jeep, Odd acceleration of his vehicle, Odd shape to his right arm, Odd man opening his door, Odd-Odd-Odd.*

Suddenly without warning Wayne's sense of humor kicks in. As the narcotics begin to claim his consciousness a thought reaches him, *how would you tell this story at a family barbecue?* All these thoughts accompany Wayne as he drifts off once again. A planned trip into oblivion hastened this time by a shot in the arm and a slow drip that hangs above his head.

* * *

Back on the roadway mail had been scattered to the wind. When the mail truck climbed the lawn before reaching the living room the rear door opened and several plastic bins of mail were delivered; just not to their intended addresses.

Hundreds of pieces of mail were picked up by a crew from the post office. They arrived a hell of a lot quicker than the man who had supposedly fixed Wayne's Jeep. Like black flies the neighborhood was flooded by do-gooders and neighbors who rubbernecked the whole event.

These same neighbors when interviewed as possible witnesses to the crash offered no help at all.

CHAPTER TWO

Wayne woke with his wife at his bedside. He met her eyes and tried to take her hand. His right arm wouldn't move. Glancing to his right he sees a cast from finger-tip to just below his shoulder. He looks to the foot of the bed where one leg, his left, is also in cast and suspended in the air from a cable.

His wife smiles tightly.

Wayne sighs deeply, hoarsely he asks, "How long have I been here?"

Becky checks her watch. She tries to use a little humor. "You are just 12 hours late for our morning coffee dear, it's 9:30 pm.

Wayne takes a deep breath. Through the pain he grimaces and offers back his wife's tight smile. "Are the girls okay?"

"They are in the waiting room chomping at the bit."

"How bad is it?"

Their relationship has always worked with nuance rather than pronouncement. Becky sees no reason to change that now.

"The doctor should be in shortly but I think it's safe to say you won't be feeding any mailboxes during this year's busy holiday season and that is months away."

Wayne shakes his head which brings on a painful wince. "I don't even know how it happened." Already in his mind he is trying to piece the story together, "Some strange shit."

It was then he tried to tell his wife the odd circumstances he experienced.

Becky frowns, not sure exactly what her husband is trying to tell her. She keeps her response vanilla, "There will be time enough later to pick the meat off that chicken we were supposed to have for dinner. Right now the girls want to see that their Dad is not in danger of going to that big post office in the sky." Her eyes mist even as she smiles.

* * *

The four ladies one after another offer tears and hugs and promises. Becky tucks in their every-day hero and the family makes their way back home. It is past 11:30 pm by the time she and the girls arrive home and wind down. Becky scoots the girls to bed telling them they do not have to go to school in the morning. They will all go to breakfast then go back to see their dad.

Becky returns to the kitchen and pours herself some Merlot and moves to the lanai, needing some alone time to process all this. She takes a sip and muses.

Wayne doesn't seem to have any permanent injuries though his arm and leg are broken pretty good. His explanation for the accident seemed odd indeed.

She sips and thinks. A smile and chuckle reaches her lips. Here alone in the dark playful humor the two employ twenty-four-seven kicks in. She imagines Wayne trying to navigate their special date with one leg and one arm. He would try. Of that she had no doubt. She chuckles aloud.

When her here and now kicks back in, real world concerns fill her mind. Insurance should cover his injuries and she is sure the Post Office must have some kind of a disability plan. She sighs, that will be the least of it.

A million other things flit through her head as the glass empties. She rises and stretches. One final sigh has her looking at the stars through the screening as a breeze makes its way through the enclosure. On this late August night Becky folds her arms and begins to shiver.

Back in the kitchen she placed the glass in the sink. Moving to lock the front door she gazes out the sidelight window to their well mowed lawn. A streetlight casts a shadow over the mailbox at the end of the drive.

Suddenly she is struck by a need to check that box. With all that has happened today, Becky hasn't checked the mail. Wayne would be disappointed if mail was left in the box overnight.

She walks down the driveway as shadows mimic her movement. She looks up and down a very quiet street. She loves her neighborhood. It has provided a safe and happy place for her family over the years. She thinks, *if I had my wine glass with me I would toast this street.*

She opens the mail box and hauls out a fist full of mail. She lets a magazine surround the pile and walks back into the house where she places it on the kitchen table. *Morning will be early enough* she reasons, *enough news for one day.* She snaps off the kitchen light and walks to the foot of the stairs where above, the girls are still yakking in various stages of hitting the (rack); a term their father uses nightly when admonishing them to, 'Climb those golden stairs.' Becky Garrett turns into the bedroom she shares with her husband.

Within a half hour the house begins to quiet. A group prayer that their dad will be okay is followed by doors closing. Darkness and silence claim their rightful place.

Becky, below, says her own silent prayers. It is strange not having her loving husband beside her in their bed. She turns and grabs Wayne's pillow to hug, *a damn poor substitute* she decides.

She smiles knowing how her husband really looks forward to their bi-weekly little 'love sessions' as he calls them, truthfully tonight she is missing them too.

The mail lays unopened on the kitchen table.

CHAPTER THREE

Wayne's alarm on the little stand at his side of the bed sounds the same time it always sounds. Becky dives across the king size bed and snaps it off.

Breathing deeply and now wide awake, she lays there thinking about Wayne waking in a bed in the hospital. She also thinks about all the short term changes that will need to happen until he is back on his feet. A deep sigh is followed by a shake of her head. Defiantly she fluffs up her pillow intending to catch a few more winks. She squeezes Wayne's pillow between her knees. She tosses and turns, sleep is not going to return. Unconsciously she begins counting on her fingers the various ways that Wayne has made life easier. When she reaches a dozen she realizes what a lucky lady she is to have him.

Watching the hands of her own alarm clock move it becomes clear there will be no more sleep. Enough is enough. A long full body stretch precedes her feet touching the floor as she rolls out of bed. She pads her way to the kitchen to start the coffee. *Wayne always does that,* she hugs herself thinking. Another thought, *while the coffee perks Wayne walks out to get the paper, place it on the table then climbs back into bed and take a minute to hug my back. More often than not he quietly whispers a lyric from a song that popped into his head in the moment. If I don't respond and offer no more than the warmth of my backside he sighs and leaves to make his own breakfast sip a coffee and be gone. Never able to get fully back to sleep with Wayne up and gone, soon she hears snatches of conversation from the girls before they too are out of the house. Eventually the smell of coffee waiting for her enters her senses and she gets up to an empty house.*

This morning though as she pours water into the coffee maker and counts out the proper measure, only half as many spoonfuls will be needed she reminds herself.

While the coffee brews she goes in to take a shower. She checks the clock, 8:15 the girls after a traumatic day are sleeping in.

On a normal day staggered alarms would have them up taking their turns in the upstairs shower. Stairs and railing would creak three separate times followed by a rustling of cereal boxes. With breakfast devoured, a slamming of the door sends them on their way to school. This morning felt like anything but normal.

She re-visits normal for a moment. *Oldest to youngest will arrive down stairs and fix their own breakfast. Becky had given up trying to plan a family breakfast years ago. While she tries to doze she catches snatches of the girls going through the teasing and giggling and slurping and sniping until the door closes on them. She lies there listening for the squeak of the bus brakes sometimes eyeing her own alarm clock, just daring it to go off. When it does she rolls out of the warm bed to begin her own daily ritual.*

This morning Becky lingered in the shower, then returned to the kitchen to bring a cup of coffee into the bathroom while she put on her face. She took a moment to look at her laugh lines. Age has deepened them but Wayne's sense of humor had put them there in the first place. *Pretty good trade off* she thought, *I'll take laugh lines and the good memories over frown lines any day,* she nods to herself in the mirror.

She will not be going in to work today so she grabs a favorite pair of jeans and a pale blue blouse. She was told visiting hours start at 10 o'clock. Becky planned to be there by nine-thirty.

The girls should be going to school since there was really nothing they could do but sit around at the hospital. But she had agreed last night on the way home they could go back in the light of day and see for themselves that Dad would mend.

Wayne would pretend to be upset that the girls changed their routine for him but Becky knew secretly he would be glad for the kidding and banter that would help him heal.

So it was that while Becky was drinking her first cup of coffee in the downstairs bathroom and musing about anything and everything she needed to do today, the girls, one by one had found their way to the kitchen. Marla had a piece of toast going by the time her sisters came on scene. Becky heard the girls arguing over the toaster and yelled out that they would be having breakfast in town in a half hour but that didn't seem to end the squabbling.

Dorothy, had just grabbed a cereal bowl and was jockeying for position in the pantry to sort through cereal choices when Marla, exclaimed, "What's all this?" Followed moments later by, "There's one for each of us."

The magazine had been opened and laid flat on the table with five envelopes spread out like blades of a fan. Each envelope was a different color. When the younger girls turned, Marla was holding her pale rose colored envelope, exclaiming, "There's no stamp and no return address. There is one envelope for each of us."

The two younger sisters descended on the table excited to have mail. "Nobody our age gets mail anymore, except maybe at Christmas," said middle child, Shellee.

"Or our birthday," squealed Dorothy, excitedly.

Shellee picked up a light turquoise envelope with her name done in the same tortured Calligraphy ink script. Her first thought was, *whoever did this needs some writing lessons.*

The youngest, Dorothy, claimed her name written on an envelope in the shade of ocean blue. She too had trouble following the wording, but it was her name for sure.

"Someone knows all our favorite colors," noted Shellee.

Their father's envelope with his name printed in pencil was slate gray; as if in mourning.

Becky Garrett's envelope was snow white with her name spelled out in pasted on irregular sized letters.

The girls were still yammering over what all this could mean and the oldest girl loudly insisting they wait for their mother before opening them. Becky hearing all the noise joined them in the kitchen.

"What are you girls arguing about now?" That was as far as she got before being handed an envelope with her name on it.

She examined the envelope. She held it to the light. She turned it over and over in her hand. *Pasted on letters. Hmmph, no post mark, no stamp, no return address.* A different thought reached her, *Wayne would be pissed. He hated when a non-postal employee opened a federally protected mail box. Someone had been in their mail.*

The girls watched their mother silently continue examining her envelope.

Finally Becky made eye contact with each girl in turn. "This is really bizarre. Let me open mine first. Your father always says, you have to be careful opening your mail these days."

Once more she held it up to the light but could not see through the envelope. She took a deep breath then using a butter knife, sliced under the flap and along the top. Not putting her hands in the envelope she held it upside down to let whatever was in there drop to the kitchen table.

Nothing fell out.

She turned to the oldest, Marla and nodded. Marla repeated her mother's efforts. Her envelope too was empty.

Shellee tried hers, nothing fluttered to the table.

Dorothy was determined that her letter would be the winner but she too was disappointed.

Only their Dad's letter remained. Becky thought for all of ten seconds before putting the knife to it. Nothing fluttered out but Becky saw several pieces of stationary visibly hugging the inside of the envelope. Gingerly she removed the paper and unfolded the first page.

With the girls wide eyed by now, Becky read the contents aloud:

> Wayne,
>
> I'm sure your wife and daughters are curious about this recent mail delivery. I'm sure they have opened your letter by now, you being laid up and all. Sorry for the lack of postage. I was in kinda of a hurry. Bet that will piss you off; being a postal worker and all.

Ladies since you are probably reading this before Wayne, I'll give you a heads up.

All of your lives are about to become much more complicated. Emptier too, like those envelopes.

Wayne, this is all on you. Look at your life. Are you sure you deserve to be this happy? Misfortune doesn't seem to stick with you. You spread happiness around like a load of manure with everyone you meet.

But Wayne if you dig deep in the shit you'll know why I'm doing this. This goes back a ways.

You probably don't remember the way back when.

But way back when happened. I was there. I watched what you did. You were greedy and selfish. I suffered for it. Unintentional though it might have been the result of your greed and selfishness changed my whole life.

You probably have no recollection of doing anything except being happy go lucky, friendly, always smiling, good old Wayne.

I have thought about the way back when at different times over the years.

I tried to let it go. Thought I had.

I've been watching you for a while now. Studying your whole family if I'm being honest. Your family all seem like bright and happy people. I survived Wayne, so part of me says let it go.

Actually it's only in the last year that you came back to mind on a regular basis. I mean I never forgot but it was only recently that your name came back up.

I read about it in the paper. You saved a kid from drowning one day at the beach. Hero Wayne, the paper called you. You got some kind of a citizen medal I read. As the saying goes, **no good deed goes unpunished** so there you have it.

My life shit the bed way back when. I realize all this seems weird and petty but since you came back to mind I can't seem to let go of it.

Misery loves company they say so we're going to conduct a little test. How much do you love your family, Wayne?

I've already put the board in the water Wayne. You laying all broken to pieces in the hospital shows you how serious I am taking this. You probably should too.

This is the back end of the hurricane season. Lately during October and November we've been hit the hardest.

When I was a kid some of the best surfing was before and after some of those storms.

But enough about me. Your own storm is rising Wayne. Are you prepared? Get your flashlights out, batten down the hatches.

On any given day things are going to cloud up for a member of your family. I won't say who it will be or what is going to happen but believe me it will cause trauma.

I lived through a lifetime of storms Wayne. One you could have stopped. In fact broken into months my storms totaled a hundred. But enough of that for now.

As a family you all just lived through Day One. I'm thinking if I took the hundred months I suffered and asked your family to live through just one day for each of the months I was in hell; that would be fair wouldn't it?

So all the sunny days you and your family have been living, well that is going to end; at least temporarily. Depends on you Wayne.

Day One is done and you, old Wayne, took the brunt of it. In time, with luck and that old post office attitude of (come rain or shine the mail must go through), maybe you can end this.

In the meantime, as you try to make sense of this; you can just call me, Hurricane Matthew.

Becky sat back speechless. Four sets of eyes met. Confusion and disbelief kept their mouths closed. Becky frowned carrying an unknowable expression. Then she spoke, "Finish breakfast here then we are heading immediately to see your dad. He'll know what to do."

*   *   *

Wayne was propped up with a doped up smile on his face.

After a series of gentle hugs, Becky took center stage. In the couples nuanced approach to problem solving she announced, "Houston we have a problem."

Wayne took the cue, tried to focus, "What's happening?"

"Before I tell you about the letters we received, walk all of us through your day yesterday. The girls haven't heard about the mechanic, the turkey, someone opening the Jeep after you crashed. Tell us anything you can remember."

Wayne, still under medication, looked confused and bemused. He was about to mildly protest when oldest daughter Marla looking spooked, spoke up, "Just do it Dad."

Wayne knew his family. Something was wrong. He took a deep breath and tried to focus. He repeated as best he could word for word what he had told Becky.

The family listened, four fertile minds drawing from the words of the letter trying to interpret what all this might mean.

When he finished, Wayne was mentally drained but asked once again, "What's happening"

Becky put a set-in cement look back on her face and told her husband of the mail delivery.

She held up a fistful of envelopes addressed to each of them. She told of opening four empty envelopes none with postage, the final one addressed to her husband.

"Yours wasn't empty." She then handed Wayne the letter that seemed to have changed their world.

Wayne was half-way through the letter trying as best he could to follow the words when a nurse entered with flowers and a big smile. "You have an admirer, Mr. Garrett, I'll just put these on this little stand." She nodded to the family members and left.

Wayne finished the letter. He could hardly remember what he had just read. He was saved from reacting when Shellee, the middle daughter, brought the card that accompanied the floral arrangement to her mother. "It's signed, Mom."

Becky read it then gasped when she read the message, "Just thinking of you, Matthew."

"My God are we being watched?"

The family turned their attention to their mother. Anger filled her eyes. "Marla go to that nurse's station and see if they know who delivered these flowers."

Wayne was still in semi-darkness about all this but one thing was becoming clear, his family was being threatened.

Somewhere in the back of his foggy brain, this letter opened a window to that past. He just had to think this all through. He tried to re-read the letter. Even as his family continued to talk around him Wayne had gone missing. He was back on the fourth floor of a tenement building, blocks from the beach.

CHAPTER FOUR

The stairs and railings to the fourth floor creaked in the wind, they creaked shrieked and groaned when carrying weight. Wayne, even as a young boy knew exactly who was on those steps at every level by the pitch of the complaint.

Just below him on floor three lived a new family recently arrived from Ohio with two children; too young to be of any use to Wayne but noisy when allowed to run in their flat.

The steps groaned, sound echoing upward as the two children were carried up and down those steps to the third floor. Once inside, sounds rose even higher into Wayne's bedroom through a floor register. These two toddlers, too small to navigate the stairs, ran rampant throughout their four room flat. The parents were equally loud in their footfalls and overheated conversation.

On the second floor lived Mr. Jensen and his wife and their tired old blind terrier, Ted. Wayne hardly ever heard them at all.

Wayne's parents were old. They didn't bound up the flights carrying anything. And as Wayne grew old enough to fetch they hardly used the stairs at all.

Wayne had no idea what having an older parent meant until he began school. The first inkling took place the evening of his first parent teacher conference. The teachers opening faux par, mistaking Wayne's mother for a grandparent, was met with nervous laughter, a course correction and an apology.

Wayne's parents didn't leave the house to go to work like other parents did, at least not in Wayne's memory. His mother was forty plus years old when Wayne was conceived.

His mother was religious, an Irish Catholic; though her attendance at church had ceased a long time ago. Wayne began to understand religion early on when never a meal passed that Gods name wasn't taken in vain.

Every complaint leveled by the man of the house, a man of strong drink and opinions. A man who took the lords name in vain at every turn, was met with a response of, "Lord forgive him."

Below on the first floor lived the owner of the building, Mr. Jamie Collins. He seemed to have the ability to hear through walls and floors. His Irish anecdotes, one liner's and stories, always carried an element of truth if you could muddle through the delivery.

On any chance meeting with his tenants, an invite would be extended to join him on the porch to sit a spell. Jamie Collins quizzed his listeners on complaints or concerns with the world at large or their flat in particular.

Inevitably he answered them with an Irish tale, quote, line, or limerick. Many of his pithy quotes, jokes, exaggerations, or made up on the spot tall tales seemed to originate from within his own mind. He was truly an Irishman.

A flag of Ireland hung just above the main entrance to the building. A zig zag of three flights of steps climbed the outside of the building to the rear of the first floor porch reaching skyward as if searching for an escape route from the blarney originating from Mr. Collins' rocking chair.

One thing was true. Mr. Jamie Collins had Irish roots deeper than the potatoes grown during the potato famine that brought his family to this country.

Also true was the fact that Jamie Collins could be a very good ally or conversely a feared enemy.

After a visit to the porch, when Wayne was hardly old enough to navigate the stairs, Wayne asked his mother what being Irish meant.

His mother set him on her knee and told Wayne stories of his own Irish roots. Stories told during long evenings they spent alone while his father, Roman Garrett, visited the local Irish Pub in downtown Flagler Beach.

From early on she told Wayne stories of Ireland's fairies, goblins, ghosts, and leprechauns. She neglected to include Ireland's history with the English, *he'll hear plenty of that from Mr. Collins I'm sure*, she reasoned.

Then along about age five just as the world was beginning to make sense everything seemed to change for Wayne. It began with a story his father brought home from the pub. A story his father repeated nightly. It began as an insinuation, one that like an unattended blister soon morphed into an accusation.

Wayne didn't have a clue what his father was talking about. But just the way his father held his mouth when telling a story that nightly gained legs, led Wayne to surmise this was not one of the funny stories his father sometimes shared.

Margaret Garrett listened with her mouth clamped tight ignoring the liquored breath, the accusations, and the digs. Every head nod of resignation held a silent, *Lord forgive him.*

Then in her own way on those evenings alone with Wayne she told her own truth. When Wayne asked his mother to explain his father's nightly outbursts she was honest with the boy. "Your father is known about town as an Irish wannabe. Truth be told he is an Englishman. There's nothing worse than a pretender in the eyes of the Irish." She left it at that for a time.

But as the insinuations continued to arrive nightly and became accusations shrouded in an Irish riddle, one night she looked Wayne in the eyes and began a history lesson. She didn't have time to wait on Jamie Collins giving Wayne his version of the bastard British.

"Our own long and troubled history with the English is filled with the British over the centuries pretending they had Irish best interests at heart; even as they went about the business of stealing our land and trying to steal our heritage."

She gave examples then finished with, "So Wayne never be a pretender. Just be who you are and live with the consequences, that's the Irish way."

From vague accusations, to pointed fingers, to cross words between his mother and father a war began to cross the kitchen table along with the passing of the peas.

Wayne, pushing his peas into a corner saving the worst for last, didn't understand any of it. The war got louder and left the table, creeping into Wayne's bedroom and finally into his sleep.

Just when Wayne was about to ask his mother to please explain all the noise in a way he could truly understand, all went to silence.

Suddenly it was as if a truce between the northern and southern Island that Jamie was schooling him on had been declared.

Suddenly it was as if his two parents didn't live in the same flat. His mother's eyes turned downward whenever the man of the house entered the room. She began to take an interest in and give full attention to crossword puzzles. In the process she began ignoring Wayne as well. These changes to his world left Wayne puzzled and confused.

His father too seemed to have developed new habits. Nightly for the first five years of Wayne's life, the man had stumbled home from the pub threw out his accusation let a fart, chuckled, and simply gone to bed.

Now suddenly his father was changing tactics. Upon his arrival he began waking and corralling Wayne plying him with his stupid Irishmen jokes that Wayne seldom caught the humor in. Wayne half-asleep, listened to drivel that seemed to be more riddle than story. Wayne was as puzzled by his father's actions as he was by his mother's silence.

Now at age seven he was ignored and confused by his mother, woken and frightened by a father bringing home more than just the smell of a pub of unwashed men, it was like he had new parents.

Wayne began to confide in the man on the porch who seemed genuinely interested in what Wayne had to say.

He told Jamie Collins that when sober, his father simply ignored him. Now he was making an appearance nightly and not going directly to bed. Wayne said he would wake with a hand on his arm shaking him. Wayne still half asleep told Jamie Collins he couldn't make sense of the stories his father was spinning.

Wayne was a smart little boy so though he might not know the meaning of the stories he could repeat them nearly word for word.

Jamie Collins hung on every word.

"No one can tell a joke like an Irishman," my father tells me nearly every night. I can't even turn my head his way he smells so bad. He must have told me nearly a hundred stories that always begins with, **two Irishmen go into a bar."**

"Lately," he told Jamie. "his father's attempt at humor always seemed to focus on how Wayne came into the family and that it was the greatest Irish Joke of all time.

'You see there was a third expected,' my father tells me time after time, 'but in the end, the third never arrived.'

"What could that mean Mr. Collins?"

Jamie Collins continued to listen.

"My father always pauses in the story and a glaze enters his eyes. Then he sighs and farts and lets the smell settle and leaves the room with a final line."

'Nine months later you showed up.' "This is the story that I am woken to nearly every night like clockwork."

Jamie Collins had an idea of what was being said but kept it to himself. A single thought entered his mind though, *Every dog has his day.*

This nightly ritual went on until Wayne caught the punch line in the birds and bees discussions on the school playground.

Wayne finally figured out how he had arrived on the fourth floor, he just didn't know who had directed traffic.

A quiet anger of not knowing what was really being said right under his nose festered in Wayne. He had no idea why he should be angry but he was not about to let on that his father's obvious abuse was getting to him.

He continued to nod, smile, and laugh in all the right places as his old man ended each story in the dark of night. He was determined to solve this mystery he told Mr. Collins.

Mr. Collins refused to speculate.

Wayne's mother, listened to the nightly rants from the kitchen table where she spent nearly her entire life now, inhabiting the shadows and the gloom. Lately new verbal assaults were added: never a meal good enough, or a wash clean enough. With each complaint she dove deeper into the mysteries of her crossword puzzles.

Time passed and a new normal set in. Wayne couldn't change things back so he adapted. Wayne loved school and he got along well there. So mostly Wayne remained a happy kid.

Though he would hardly be considered a kid since he now did all the shopping for food and brought home any required medicines, climbing the flights holding tight to paper bags that seemed to shift at each step.

The only product that entered not bearing Wayne's finger prints was his father's whiskey.

Mostly that came from the only visitor to the flat, a gray little man with hardly any teeth and a bleached out comb over.

On occasion the building's owner, Jamie Collins, would stop Wayne on his way in and ask him to bring a bottle to his father. Knowing how liquor affected his father Wayne didn't like doing that but he did it anyway.

Jamie Collins had a reason to keep Roman liquored up but he didn't share that with Wayne.

Roman Garrett also no longer left the flat. He had been banned from the pub for a while now for starting a row he couldn't finish.

His mother broke her silence long enough to tell Wayne one night after Roman had passed out, "If you are going to pick a fight with an Irishman you better have the stamina to finish the job."

Roman ripe and wounded had been unceremoniously dropped on the first floor porch in the wee hours of a Saturday morning.

Jamie Collins nearly tripped over him on his way to retrieve the morning paper. He shook his head knowingly and left Roman lying there in his own mess.

From that night on Roman Garrett didn't leave his flat. Wayne watched his father lick his wounds shouting to the sky of how he had been jumped by a half dozen or more.

So Wayne began shopping for groceries and Jamie Collins began sending up a bottle, though a lot less often than Roman would have liked.

The same message was always delivered with the bottle. Mr. Collins made Wayne repeat the lines till he had them down pat. 'Roman, may you always have walls for the winds and a roof for the rains.' The message held a warning that Wayne was not privy to.

When he handed his father the bottle and dutifully recited his lines his father would turn black in the face; he always accepted the bottle though. His mother remained quiet with her eyes on her puzzle.

Wayne couldn't remember a time he hadn't lived here. By the time he reached the age of nine he had traveled the three flights to the fourth floor (to his mind) a hundred million times.

* * *

Tired from the nearly one mile walk to the grocery, and relieved that Mr. Collins was not on his porch to offer an opinion, he climbed those damn groaning steps with a grocery bag tucked and balanced under each arm and entered the kitchen on the fourth floor; breathless. He set the two paper bags noisily on the table.

His mother was sitting there squinting, doing one of her cross word puzzles, a magnifying glass held an inch from the clues. She didn't look up, knowing if she didn't acknowledge her son he would put the groceries away. It was as if she had given up on life.

Wayne sat down heavily at the table. Looking over the grocery bags he studied his mother. He innocently asked a question. "Mom, why do we have to live on the fourth floor? We have been here longer than anyone else. Couldn't we move down stairs when someone moves out?"

Sometimes his mother spoke in riddles as confusing as his old man or Jamie Collins even. She raised her eyes as if noticing him for the first time in a long time. She took a deep breath and managed, "To be in the building at all is an act of kindness, fostered by a fondness for you yourself."

Wayne sat there trying to digest what had just been said.

His father, awake, listening, and unhappily sober was spoiling for a fight. He emerged from the bedroom, hair all askew, stained underpants sagging, eyes blazing. He crossed the kitchen and glanced out the window as if in thought. Then he cleared his throat and spit loudly in the sink. He turned and glared at his wife. There was no drink in the house and none had arrived from below which further infuriated him.

He cleared his throat once more and loudly announced, "Oh we pay a rent. Don't let your mother fool you. A hundred times over we pay for this little bit of heaven, don't we **dear**?" He turned and spat once more. Without further comment, a creature of horrible habits he broke wind and removed himself from the stink, letting his words ride the odor. This was the day to day life Wayne lived.

* * *

Things remained about the same above, below, and around the four story building that like the steps, swayed and squeaked and squawked, and groaned in the weather for the next three years. Somehow Wayne remained cheerful, filling his head with books that always had a happy ending. All the kids at school loved Wayne. He was always upbeat and friendly and helpful.

* * *

Today was Wayne's Twelfth Birthday. He hurried home from school hoping for a great big Chocolate cake and ice cream with candles to blow out, sitting right next to a wrapped present he had been asking for.

Mr. Jamie Collins met him on the first step.

"You're getting big, Wayne, 12 years old today is it?"

"Yes sir, today's the day."

"Have you started that paper route I told you about? Haven't heard those steps squeaking in the early morning dark."

"Monday morning sir. I have walked the route with my supervisor. So Monday morning."

Then Mr. Jamie Collins said something odd. "You will be the man of the house. I'm very proud of you."

Wayne didn't know what to say. He stammered, "Well I guess I ought to get up there and celebrate."

"Before you go, I have something for you."

He must have been waiting for me? thought Wayne. Mr. Jamie Collins reached into his pocket and removed a small square box.

He handed Wayne the box, looked at him and smiled.

Wayne opened the box. A gold ring with a crest of some kind covered the front. Wayne looked at Mr. Jamie Collins for explanation.

"Did you know your Mother is Irish? Of course you did." Before Wayne could respond Mr. Collins continued, "Her family lived in the same neighborhood as mine growing up. We Irish have to stick together." He pointed, "That ring was handed down in my family from 200 years ago. That crest you see is my family's coat of arms, it has quite the history." He pointed to a rocker. "Sit a moment."

Jamie seated himself then began to recite something he'd either heard or written himself. He was always quoting something to Wayne.

"From soldier to sailor, tinker to tailor,

Even a whaler if you can believe.

Mined from a river its protection delivered

All written down in our family screed."

He smiled to himself and continued, "This ring from the County of Cork in Ireland, will provide you a safe harbor on those cold dark mornings you are soon to enter."

He raised his eyes then, "There is just one thing I ask. Don't show the ring about. It is very rare and valuable. Certainly don't show your father for he'd sell it off for a bottle of cheap whiskey."

Wayne wasn't sure how to respond but nodded his head and put the ring in his pocket.

Mr. Jamie Collins dismissed him with a wave and an odd glisten in his eyes. *Actually tearing up* thought Wayne.

The remainder of the birthday didn't go near as well.

His father somehow had come across a bottle. The somehow was sitting in the shadows of the kitchen. Wayne smelled him before he saw him. The only friend from Roman's days at the pub had shown up.

Wayne had never liked the look or the smell of him. He had a bleached out comb-over that ran this way and that. The next feature that emerged was a nearly toothless mouth that spewed filthy talk in every sentence uttered. It was obvious from his smell that he bathed with the same frequency he brushed his few remaining teeth or combed his hair.

Wayne was shocked that his mother even allowed him into their home.

The first question his father asked each time the dirty little man arrived was, "Jamie Collins didn't see you did he?"

"I can still navigate a friggin rogue wave when I need to, don't you be bothering your ass about him. I lived here long enough to learn all the ways to avoid the son of a bitch."

He was sitting here now at the table drinking with Wayne's bleary eyed father, describing in the coarsest of terms how he used to ride a twenty foot wave to hell and back. 'The girls watching from the beach will let you ride them with the same determination.' Both men snickered into their cups.

Wayne's mother remained out of ear shot in the bedroom.

The cake sat silently on the sideboard awaiting the celebration.

Wayne fingered the ring in his pocket still confused as to why Mr. Jamie Collins had given him such a valuable present.

His mother joined them in the kitchen lit the candles and sang happy birthday to him. Wayne blew out the 12 candles. Wayne's father and his friend talked loudly through the whole ceremony.

Three pair of eyes watched the unwrapping of a much simpler but more practical gift than the one offered on the porch. A new jacket with a hood that would keep Wayne warm on those early morning paper deliveries.

It was the one he had picked out from a magazine he had shown his mother. *So she does hear me at times*, thought Wayne. The mail had come through. Wayne put the jacket on, preening into the mirror over the sink.

His father of English descent, but a good faker spoke up, slurring his words, "Don't get ahead of yourself with your strutting, that's been the curse of the Irish for centuries."

His father's friend cackled and held up his glass. "Get cocky on a wave and you'll end up flat on your ass chewing sand."

Wayne had no idea what his father or this fellow drunkard was talking about.

Wayne's mother was not about to let her husband ruin her son's birthday. She pointed first to the surfer dude. "Close your dirty mouth or you'll be swallowing the entire sea bed."

Then she met her husband's eyes. "Roman, let all your evil thoughts settle for this one day, I'm asking."

She stood and placed her hands on Wayne's shoulders. "The boy became a man today and starting Monday morning he'll be doing a man's work. So let the boy be."

Roman's friend toasted that remark, bit back a rejoinder with his lips curled fighting the urge, but kept his filthy mouth shut.

Roman Garrett, who couldn't win a battle at the bar thought to win this one at home. He stood weaving already lost in the storm but returned the volley. "Since he's a man now," he stammered, "maybe you can explain to him that story I 've been telling him for years. The one he seems too dense to understand." He toasted his friend who had heard that same story at the pub. They both smirked.

Margaret Garrett had had enough. "Okay Roman, let's take the gloves off, let this cat out of the bag." That quieted the kitchen. She stood looking at her husband, tears welling up in her eyes.

She turned to his friend, "And don't you dare raise that glass or I'll fill that toothless mouth with it. Then she turned to her son.

"You see son, your father insists the man down stairs, the man you know as Mr. Jamie Collins tip-toed up these stairs on a dark and stormy night while your father was in his cups at the local distillery."

She turned back toward her husband but continued to talk directly to her son. "Your father doesn't recall crawling those stairs himself and forcing himself on me."

With wide eyes tearing up, the words kept coming, "Hurting me. Bloodying me." A deep breath followed, she wasn't done. "Easier to swallow that a man of principle, Mr. Jamie Collins, took advantage of me."

She crossed her arms as she moved to the window and looked down on a bleak landscape. In the distance she could see steam escaping the mighty Atlantic. Her own anger waned. She waited, just daring a response.

The mouth of Roman's friend stayed closed. His glass remained on the table.

Finally Roman Garrett rose, his head hanging, knowing the truth of it. He had fired his final volley and once again, just as in his bar fights, the enemy stood unharmed.

Even more concerning he had run out of Irish stories to hold over Margaret. More damning still was the knowledge that Margaret had spoken a truth that would hold.

All these years Margaret had sought to protect her son from such an accusation and suffered Roman's terrible looks and taunts and teases. On this very night, with her son on the threshold of adult hood, Margaret had chosen to speak the truth.

Where would Roman's fabled Irishmen go from here to spin a yarn? What liquored up limerick was left to poison the air? A heavy air hung just below the kitchen light.

Roman moved in slow motion putting on his jacket, tattered and torn. Like a child being sent to his room he put a pout on his face, grabbed his bottle and his friend and just like Elvis; Roman Garrett left the building.

With the slamming of the door and the creaking of the stairs, Mother and son were left to eat cake. Wayne had not moved a muscle. Now after a tearful embrace of the truth, Wayne pulled out the ring and showed his mother. She nodded her approval. "Just don't show that ring to your father."

"That's what Mr. Collins said."

She cleared the table and her throat, "Everything I told you tonight is true. What I haven't told you is also true. Let me just make a cup of tea." With a nervous hand dipping a tea bag she began. "Mr. Jamie Collins in a different story could indeed have been your father."

Wayne remained confused.

"If I'd had more sense and patience we would be living on the first floor." She removed the tea bag, rising and placing it in the garbage. She took Wayne's empty plate and cut another piece of what was supposed to be a celebration cake. When they were sitting across from one another Wayne's question, posed a long while ago, was addressed. "You asked me once why we have to live up on the fourth floor. It's time you heard that story."

Wayne fortified himself by shoveling a second helping of cake into his mouth.

Margaret breathed in steam from the tea, "I grew up in the same neighborhood as Jamie Collins." She sipped. "He wasn't a Mr. Collins back then, just a handsome boy with a bright future." She sipped once more. "His family had a bit of money."

Then she changed course slightly. "Do you remember me reminding you over and over when you asked for something we couldn't afford that <u>if wishes were horses then beggars could ride</u>." She studied the liquid. "My own family lived on those wishes. "Never did get a damn horse." She chuckled. "Anyway, Jamie and I became fast friends all through school." A sudden smile crossed her face, "We actually became close enough so that promises were made to one another."

She nodded her head remembering, "Promises that were empty wishes, my mother reminded me when I didn't date anyone else with Jamie gone off to College. My mother's scolds turned into a cascade of derisive laughter when Jamie didn't return after college but joined the armed forces instead."

She took a deep breath, not used to all this talk. "Meanwhile Roman Garrett had come to town." She hmmphed, "He was a dazzler back then. All black hair and blue eyes and those same promises. On a high horse of his own or so it seemed. Still I resisted." Margaret rolled her eyes, "My mother though continued to peck at me. 'A bird in the hand is worth two in the bush', she pecked. "I can still see her pointing finger directly under my nose; peck peck peck."

She rose to look back out at the dark of night. Seconds passed then she continued, "Finally I relented." A sigh of complicity followed. "I give your father credit he put on quite a show at first. Maybe my mother was right I began to think."

A million reasons that proved the falsehood of that belief filtered through her mind.

"But in the end Roman Garrett turned out to be one of those crazy little birds that feign injury." She closed her eyes trying to put a name to them. "You know that bird that limps and flops to keep others away from its nest, though they rarely spend time there themselves. You've seen them on the lawn, weaving this way and that just like your father after time with the drink." She paused and thought a minute, "Killdeer, yes that's what they are named. That's what your father was and is, a damn crazy bird."

One final deep breath allowed Margaret to finish, "It's often said that to hasten an Irish story is considered a sin." She chuckled but her words carried no mirth. "To finally answer your question of why we live on the top floor; while Mr. Jamie Collins and I can't be and have never been together, we do still love one another."

She had to get up and move about. "Even now after all this time I swear if there was less than three floors between us I'd most likely venture down. The man loves you as his own Wayne, because in our hearts you are his own."

Wayne had listened without words. He was numb.

"Welcome to manhood son, life can be complicated." She rose to freshen her tea. "My mother was right, if wishes were horses this beggar would be living a lot closer to the ground. Go get some sleep now son. Morning comes early as you'll find out Monday next."

My father didn't come home that night. Nor the next. Nor the next month nor the next year. Occasionally I would see his friend weaving the streets of Flagler Beach then after a time he disappeared too. I would never see my father again. Rumors had him drowned, murdered, or just drunk somewhere as close as one town over even.

One rumor which most likely held no merit emerged when a fire broke out in the basement of our building. It was during the first months of my father's disappearance. The fire was quickly discovered and little damage took place. When the Fire chief investigated it seemed someone had been attempting to live down there. The only clue was an empty whiskey bottle.

There seemed little interest regarding his absence and the building on Tilbury Street, four blocks back from the beach creaking and complaining in the wind, stayed silent on the matter of Roman Garrett's disappearance. In the back of my mind I always wondered what Mr. Jamie Collins knew of it all. We never discussed it.

CHAPTER FIVE

The two youngest girls sat across from one another at the foot of their father's bed while Becky and Marla framed a sleeping Wayne at the top. Wayne stirred and came awake. Four pair of eyes were staring at him, he was confused.

"Welcome back from the dead. You were gone for more than half an hour."

Surrounded by the women he held most dear he shook away sleep and those early memories he had been visiting. His eyes widened as he rejoined the present.

The women remained silent as if waiting for an answer to this mystery.

"I have no idea what this is all about." He sighed deeply, his eyes widened, "Obviously, there is a crazy person out there. We should call the police." The girls nodded their heads in agreement.

"Let's think this through. First." Becky held up a finger. "What are we going to tell them?" She began to tick off what sounded like a crazy story. " A broken Jeep, a mechanic who is gone when you get back, a wild turkey running in front of you, a racing engine, brakes that don't work, someone opening your door." Exasperated, her eyes met each of her daughters.

"I mean we can show them the letter but what then?" She shook her head, "They will think we're nut cases."

"But mom we have to do something this is scary," said Marla.

Becky nodded, still thinking. "Wayne you say you didn't recognize the man in the mail truck?"

"I didn't get a good look at the man no, but something in the back of my mind tells me I might have seen him before I just can't put my finger on it."

"Would you recognize the man if you saw him again?"

"Probably not."

Becky rose. "We will figure this out. "We'll be back." Wayne watched his family leave. All this had tired him out and he closed his eyes, not to sleep but to try to solve this at its roots.

CHAPTER SIX

It was still dark when Wayne's mother shook him awake. "Get dressed, I'll make you some Cocoa."

Wayne stumbled into jeans a tee shirt and a sweater. He rubbed his eyes and went to the kitchen. He checked the time. It was early yet.

"There's time for that cocoa and a piece of toast."

When his father went down those steps on Wayne's birthday his mother intuited he wasn't coming back.

Over the weekend she seemed to come back alive. The rugs were shampooed, the couch covers and sheets were washed, doors and windows opened to the air. It seemed Margaret Garrett was washing and airing that man right out of her life.

Wayne didn't truly understand what had caused all this, he was just glad to have his mother back. Wayne finished his toast and cocoa and put on his new jacket and a stocking cap, then it still being early he laid on the floor staring up at the kitchen light.

He listened to his mother humming softly. The smell of fresh toast lingered and Wayne hugged himself feeling comforted for the first time in a long time. He mentally began walking his paper route. He just knew this first job would be successful.

When his mother announced, "its time," he rose, hugged his mother and started down the stairs. When he got to the first floor the darkness spoke.

"Watch out for skunks of all description lad, and put every paper in its proper location." Mr. Jamie Collins emerged from the night. "Remember son the Irish are depending on you."

Wayne nodded then skipped off the porch and began his trek to the plant where the papers had already been dropped off. His job would require filling two canvas carriers with papers then throw straps across opposite shoulders then begin his walk of a dozen streets 'delivering the good news,' his supervisor had told him.

* * *

In the first month on the job Wayne found that delivering the papers became the easy part of the job. The hard part was collecting payment when due and possible tips.

Every Saturday beginning at 9:00 am, Wayne repeated his early morning route hoping to see an envelope in the door or on the stoop. Wayne had seventy-five customers, more promised in the future if he did the job properly.

In any given week in addition to the weekly cost of the paper he might be tipped a total of twelve to fifteen dollars from his customers. The books had to balance. Monday afternoon he had to turn in the bill for all those papers, paid in full.

If Wayne couldn't collect from someone in a given week he had to use some of his tip money to make up the difference. When no envelope showed its face in a doorway or pinned to the mail box he had to go back a second or even third time.

Sometimes a light would be on and he could collect on the morning of a delivery. Wayne learned not to be shy he had become a businessman.

Wayne found Mr. Jamie Collins, who always seemed to be out on his porch when he returned, to be a good listener. Coming back home after Saturday collections, he would pull up a rocker let out a deep sigh and the two would compare notes.

"Mr. Findlay is never home. He owes me for three weeks now. I've gone back three times. And his light is never on in the morning," complained Wayne.

"Have you left a note with the paper?"

"Twice."

Mr. Jamie Collins cupped his chin. "I know Mr. Findlay a little, I'll talk with him."

He chuckled then, "I'll let him know you're footing his bill. He won't like it put like that."

And so things got better. Every customer who forgot to put the money out, if it became a regular occurrence, was reminded by Mr. Jamie Collins of how they were letting the boy down.

Wayne ended up keeping his paper route right through High school and added another fifty papers to boot. Tips had grown over the years as Mr. Jamie Collins offered Wayne's customers his own special kind of encouragement.

It seemed, silently and with little fanfare, Mr. Jamie Collins had entered all parts of Wayne's life.

When Wayne walked across the stage to receive his high school diploma, his mother and Mr. Jamie Collins sat in the audience, three seats apart. His father was still missing.

CHAPTER SEVEN

Wayne remained in the hospital for two weeks. When he could take a dozen steps and navigate a bathroom visit he was taken to a rehab facility.

During that week the family visited daily. Becky had visited what she deemed the scene of the crime knocking on doors trying to find a possible witness. She had visited Wayne's employer and was assured no mail truck had responded to Wayne's plight. "How is that possible?" she asked.

"We got his message alright but we still hadn't made arrangements when the news reached us of the accident."

Becky left shaking her head in disbelief.

On the ninth day of this calendar of worry the family was struck by a second gut punch to the family; though Becky didn't recognize it as such immediately.

It began when she tried to fill her gas tank. Her card was denied. Becky who was careful to a fault with finances, went inside to the attendant and asked him if he would try her card again. "There must be some mistake."

A second effort mirrored the first. Becky sighed, left the gas mart and checked her watch. She removed her car from the gas pumps, parked and scrolled through her contact list. When finished she walked across the street to where her daughters were waiting, perusing a fast food menu.

She reached into her wallet handing a twenty dollar bill to her daughter. She smiled tightly and said, "Go ahead, just order me a Chicken Wrap I need to make a call."

As the girls stood in line making their own menu choices Becky stood just outside waiting to get beyond all the banks' menu choices.

The girls wandered to find a table. Becky finally got a live voice. She explained the bank debit card denial, not hiding her frustration.

The voice on the other end of the phone promised to look into it and put Becky on hold. Elevator music filled Becky's ear. Miracle of miracles, it didn't take long.

"I'm sorry ma'am your account shows a ten dollar balance. I see that you don't carry an overdraft provision so your card was appropriately denied."

Becky was shell shocked. "I will be at the bank in an hour. Could you please set up an appointment with a supervisor? There has obviously been some mistake." She heard her own voice rising and took a breath to calm down. "There should be over three thousand dollars in my checking account." Becky hung up and went in to have lunch with her daughters. She still was not making the connection but had lost her appetite, barely picking at her meal.

An hour later with the girls delivered home she sat across from a very knowledgeable bank employee.

"Someone with all your banking information, using your digital identification withdrew all but ten dollars from your account."

"They left ten dollars?"

"Just enough to keep the account open for thirty days and not trigger a call from us. I see that you don't have a savings account with us. I would suggest wherever you save, you might want to check those accounts."

Becky sat back, mouth hanging open, "What can I do?"

"It sounds like you have been hacked. We can start a fraud investigation immediately but it will take time. I also should caution you that you might not be able to recover your money. A debit card is just like money."

The lady raised her brow. I would also suggest you use a credit card rather than a debit card. It's harder to steal your money and if you do get hacked we can put a hold on any transactions you question while we investigate."

Becky's head was spinning. She needed to talk to Wayne. She exited the bank with her head on a swivel wondering even then if she might be being watched. She studied her eyes in the rearview mirror, sighing deeply. She opened her purse and removed her final twenty dollar bill to fuel the gas tank.

An hour later she was waiting just outside the glass window watching her husband go through his rehab routine. *He sure was working hard.* Her phone buzzed.

Marla's picture appeared on the screen, Becky answered.

Marla didn't wait for her mother to speak. "Mom there's another letter."

CHAPTER EIGHT

Aerial Ambrose Steward stood looking in the mirror. In his reflection he could see the window behind him. Another beautiful late summer day in Flagler Beach, Florida beckoned him. He had only recently returned to this little beach town.

He looked at himself full on. Thin, gaunt, scarred, and haunted would best describe the fifty four year old man looking back at him. He sighed deeply.

At that moment his sister hollered that breakfast was ready. He had been up and at it for hours now. He was more than ready for food.

He entered the kitchen of a small trailer located on a side street well back from the water in Flagler Beach. His sister remained seated. She looked worse than he did if you could believe it. His father had died and word had reached him. Now half of this little piece of heaven belonged to him. He looked across the table at a sister who didn't look like she should be buying green bananas.

Aerial, had been aptly named by his now deceased surfer dude father. AERIAL: <u>a surfer's term for leaving the surface of a wave</u>, always seemed to be hovering over the real world. He had spent a good number of years away from that real world; either on the water or locked up in one jail or another up and down the eastern seaboard.

He wasn't bad enough to warrant prison nor good enough to walk free; rather he hovered as his name (Aerial) implied.

He joined his sister, Bailing at the table. Her wheel chair was pulled up close. Her lap was covered with food crumbs. She clumsily spooned a bowl of oatmeal smothered in sugar into a mouth that didn't quite close. Her hands shook while her eyes showed no light. (Bailing) another surfing term that had her living up to her name. Her father a drunkard and abuser and a wise ass to boot, had somehow come up with names for his kids that seemed almost prescient. BAILING: <u>a surfing term for one who leaves their surfboard early to avoid a wipe out.</u>

Bailing had spent nearly her full fifty years leaving the party early so to speak.

From the time she could talk she conjured up excuses; she needed to be carried, her legs were tired, her room was always a mess, homework was forever left unfinished. She refused to help out. She would never feed the dog.

At a personal level she was just as lax in her personal hygiene. Up and down the block everyone knew Bailing Steward. Her name brought to mind a single word; Sloth.

Bailing would argue that the one time she tried to fit in, and actually tried to get the boys to slow down and take her home, was what put her permanently in a chair she had to navigate twenty-four seven.

Three boys, classmates but never friends, had been drinking heavily. They spotted Bailing walking aimlessly along A1A hugging the shadows. When they spoke from the passenger window, Bailing expecting to hear abuse heaped on her, moved to the shadows on the sidewalk. Just another Saturday night alone for Bailing.

When the abuse didn't come and a friendly voice enticed her to come to the window, Bailing just couldn't resist.

A beer was thrust out the window along with an invitation to join them for a ride along the ocean, Bailing took the bait. They pulled off onto one of the side streets which ended up in a local park. When a second beer had been consumed, hard liquor made an appearance. Then the playful touching began. Bailing barely conscious tried unsuccessfully to end this. Play turned to abuse as each boy in turn took their turn. Holding their nose while ribbing each other, round two about to begin. Bailing suddenly threw up.

The boys immediately lost interest and when Bailing began wailing like only Bailing could, they became a little frightened. The driver decided that they needed to let some time pass and think this all through before dumping Bailing back in town.

During this ride Bailing came full awake and really started making a fuss. Screaming at the top of her lungs the things her father would do to the boys, the trouble they were in. **"Take me home!"**

Her wailing and blubbering caused such a distraction that the driver lost control and crashed.

In the aftermath the only punishment the boys received came from their friends who razzed them for lowering themselves in the first place.

Aerial poured a second cup of coffee.

"So what you gonna do on such a beautiful day brother?" she managed between mouth-fulls and spillage. "Other than wreak havoc that is," she choked out.

Aerial took a long look at this sister. "Well Bailing, let me tell you what I plan to do. I'm going to catch a couple of waves at the big watering hole then probably hunker down in a smaller one and drink the liquid instead of riding it."

Aerial sat back, smirked and took another hard look at his sister. "And you I suppose will spend the day doing wheelies up and down the driveway, right? Between meals that is."

Bailing gave her brother a dirty look, "Smart ass."

"You should be thanking me for getting you out of that nursing home not giving me grief."

CHAPTER NINE

"Do you want me to open it?"

Becky held the phone next to her ear and waved at her husband as he continued to exert himself. *He was game that's for sure.*

She made the decision in the moment not to tell Wayne about the debit card. She was glad she hadn't barged right in and added to the man's problems, she would figure this all out. She was still trying to reach a live person at the bank that contained their savings. Now this call from Marla.

"Go ahead, I'm listening."

Marla began,

"Dear Garrett family, I am sorry to inform you that all of your disposable income has been compromised. You probably already know that. Don't worry it's safe with me, ha ha. I watched Wayne recently going through his rehab like a wild man.

Wayne still seems to have his positive can-do attitude. Let's see if we can change that. Life isn't always a day at the beach. Course he didn't do much of that fun stuff anyway, he was always delivering those damn papers.''

Matthew

Wayne returned to his room exhausted and wrung out like a dish towel. Becky joined him. Weighing in her mind whether she should add to what the man had to lift.

Wayne could read her eyes though and when he asked she answered.

"All our money is missing!"

Wayne's eyes widened

Becky held up her hand, "In our checking at least." Becky was not one to panic but she was obviously shaken. She sighed deeply and continued, "Marla just read me a letter over the phone from this creep. He's watching us and laughing at us."

Wayne tossed his head side to side trying to absorb what this all meant, "What does the letter say? Call her back I want to hear what he said."

Wayne listened as his daughter read word for word the toxic message. Wayne's mind had cleared in the last week and he listened carefully.

He had reread the earlier correspondence and determined this had to be someone from his past. How far back he needed to go he wasn't sure but if this letter offered a clue, it seemed he knew this person as a kid, a teenager at least. This latest message mentioned his paper route and the beach. What the hell?

Becky watched him as he silently mulled this over.

Wayne hoarsely cleared his throat, "Go ahead honey and check in on our savings with the bank." His eyes closed briefly, "Keep the girls safe. You be safe. I'm so sorry this is happening but we'll figure this out."

Even as Becky closed the door to her husband's room Wayne turned his head to the window.

* * *

Becky did sit before a bank official who suggested Becky file a claim that the security arm of the bank would investigate. No promises were made, no apologies given and Becky left the bank thinking her family's twelve year relationship with the bank seemed not to matter. She left thinking the bank saw her only as a series of numbers on the bottom of a check.

* * *

Wayne sat on a stool in the shower at the rehab facility, one arm and a leg draped in plastic. While water cascaded onto his upturned face the warmth of the water reminded him of the days from his youth. Despite what the letter indicated he had enjoyed the warm waters off Flagler Beach on mid-summer afternoons, a welcome respite from spending the morning delivering papers. Once more he drifted back.

CHAPTER TEN

In surfing terms (**gnarly** <u>refers to heavy, big, and dangerous surf. Extreme conditions.</u>

In a small trailer on the outskirts of town in Flagler Beach, Florida, the term gnarly would best describe the environment inside that rusted out tin can.

The year is 1980. Aerial Steward has just been ordered to get a damn job. "You're old enough to help out for Christ's sake."

The words spilling over the table left the mouth of a man who hadn't held a real job in all the years his son had been on earth.

Aerial opened his own mouth only to have his father drown him out with further invective.

"Don't even start with me. Just do it. You're man grown for Christ's sake." He pointed in the direction of the mighty Atlantic. "That damn beach isn't going to put food on the table unless its fishing you're doing, not standing on a board. If it's fishing, then you need to change your bait cause nothing is appearing on my dinner table you little shit."

A fork hit Aerial in the chest. "You're making me look bad with my buddy. From what I hear his kid is already working a job and he's younger than you."

Blurry eyes dared a reaction to either the fork or the words. With words as wet as mist hitting the air when a wave crashes over a rock the old man was dispensing Spittle.

Aerial Steward stared in silence. He knew if he said anything a fist would follow his father's words. He looked at his sister who occupied the third chair around the kitchen table. She lowered her eyes while she chewed. She was always lowering her eyes, she was always chewing. The kids' mother sat in the bathroom with a towel over her eyes and ears.

Aerial dragged his chair away from the table, rose and turned to leave. Making sure he was out of firing range he took a deep breath, "Okay old man I'll find work."

* * *

Not that far away Wayne Garrett had hours ago risen to make his paper delivery. He had been at it for over a month. He enjoyed the peacefulness of the early part of the day.

Several streets on his route ended at Route A1A. The smells and sounds of the ocean creeped up over the scrub as the mighty Atlantic washed and rinsed itself, promising a clean start to the morning. Wayne took a deep breath filling himself.

This afternoon he would be meeting with his supervisor. Additional customers might be available. One of the other carriers had quit and Wayne was the front runner to pick up another fifty deliveries.

* * *

Aerial Steward late this same afternoon, after a morning of surfing and wasting time, found his way to that same supervisor. A boy Aerial recognized was on his way out of the building, whistling.

Aerial entered the small office of the Flagler County satellite location for the News Journal. It was more of a closet really but it had a desk and a man sitting behind it.

Palmer Higgins wore several hats. He drummed up advertising for the paper and he served as circulation manager. He invited Aerial to sit down. "How can I help you?"

Aerial, not a waster of words simply said, "I need a job."

Palmer Higgins, a man educated beyond his intelligence loved the opportunity to have power over a situation and relished milking it for all its worth. He suggested Aerial tell him all about himself.

Aerial didn't have the words. "What do you mean? I'm here and I need a job."

"Certainly you have a past, present, and if this goes well perhaps even a future with our company. What experiences are you bringing in the door with you?"

Aerial asked himself, *who is this guy?* But he tried. "I'm sixteen years old. I live in town. I need a job. I heard at the beach one of your paper boys quit. That's why I'm here."

"Well yes, there was an opening but I believe we have already filled it with a competent candidate."

"I really need this job."

"Unfortunately your competition has already proven himself on the job and applied earlier. If you care to fill out an application I will consider you for the future." Palmer Higgins rose, handed

Aerial an application and with a sweep of his hand invited the boy to leave his office.

Aerial was left standing on the sidewalk across from the ocean. He crossed and stood looking out over the water. He watched what he dubbed, 'beach birds' flitting along the water but scampering away just in time to avoid getting wet. A thought reached and was played out in his mind, his father's voice reaching him, '*Well take the damn job away from the kid. Not a damn thing is free in this world you gotta just take it.*' Aerial crumpled and tossed the application.

* * *

Wayne delivered his regular route this morning beginning a half hour earlier than normal. He finished his route then picked up a second stack of fifty papers and started off in the direction of down town.

This new route included downtown businesses and renters who lived over these businesses, several office buildings. and a bank. He could hear the waves lapping the shore across the street. The morning sun was just now teasing an appearance and the waves off shore gleamed white; an invitation to come play. Wayne wasn't much of a surfer but he sure enjoyed trying when time allowed.

The horizon had turned pink promising more vibrant colors to follow.

When he finished his route, which ended a quarter mile north of the pier, he crossed A1A and stood looking out over the mighty Atlantic. Several surfers were already on the water. Wayne took off his shoes and chased the little birds who remained just out of his reach. Laughing and being a kid he made his way down the beach toward his home south of the pier.

When he reached the pier he climbed up the sand walkway to get back on pavement. A series of long wooden tables used by early morning risers and frequented as well by the homeless and tourist alike were vacant this morning. Then he spotted a single boy, one he knew only by sight usually on a surf board, sitting on a bench. The boy looked up when Wayne reached the bench.

The boy spoke first. "So you're the guy who got the new route? I kinda thought it must be you."

Wayne was confused by the question but answered in a straight forward manner. "Yeah I did. I just added more papers to my other route." Wayne moved to introduce himself.

The older boy held up his hand like a stop sign. "That should have been my route."

Wayne had no words.

The boy continued, "I need this job. It's the perfect job for me really. So any chance you let it go?"

"I'm sorry, I need this job too."

Aerial nodded his head having already anticipated the answer. "My old man is pushing me to get a job. You already have one. I talked with your boss. If you give it up, I get it."

He paused, "Tell you what. I've seen you trying to stand on that piece of shit wooden board. You give me this job and I'll keep you from drowning yourself. Deal?"

Wayne was struck by the logic this kid was employing. From what he had seen of the world it was first come first served. And he didn't think Aerial Steward would be much of a teacher at any rate.

Thinking to change the subject Wayne said, "I think your sister is in my class. Bailing, right?"

Aerial sighed, "Yeah she's my sister. And you are Wayne, happy face, Garrett. I still need this job."

Wayne ended the conversation by simply saying, "I'm sorry but the job is mine." He walked away.

Ten yards down the sidewalk Aerial's voice reached him. "Surfing isn't easy is it?" He didn't wait for an answer. "Mother Nature can be a bitch Wayne. Same goes for everything else. Your life can turn on a dime."

Wayne was left to ponder what Mother Nature had to do with anything as he made his way home.

*　*　*

Wayne kept the new route but lately it wasn't anywhere near enjoyable.

For the past month Patrons were calling the business office complaining that the paper wasn't there when they arrived to open their business or office.

Wayne couldn't figure it out. He confided his frustration to his supervisor and when nothing changed he spoke to Mr. Jamie Collins one afternoon on the porch.

As usual Mr. Collins spoke in less than a straight forward manner. "It's easy to be sociable until a man finds a cow in his garden, Wayne."

Wayne, who had listened to the man address simple questions with responses dressed in outlandish clothes for years, gave him a blank look.

"You need to find the breach in the gate lad. When and how is the cow arriving?"

Seeing that Wayne's look continued to show confusion he added, "This problem calls for surveillance. Let's think this through."

They set a trap. Mr. Collins dressed as a tourist complete with sunglasses and a floppy hat, hung out at the pier nursing coffee waiting for the sun to rise in the east. He watched Wayne deliver the papers to that side of town.

It didn't take long for Mr. Collin's cow to emerge. He nodded to himself. He knew this boy.

Aerial Steward in the near light of day picked up several of the papers Wayne had delivered then disappeared behind a building.

When Wayne arrived later that day to Mr. Collins' porch Mr. Collins once more spoke in his special way. "The man who has luck in the morning has luck in the afternoon."

Wayne waited for the shoe to drop.

"I can identify the culprit but it's up to you to expose him. The boy's family has lived on the margins for years. Lived in this very building for a time. It seems the son has been enlisted to continue the deviltry."

When the name Aerial Steward was finally revealed, Wayne told Mr. Collins of his earlier confrontation when he first acquired the route. He was encouraged to manage the matter.

Wayne went back to his boss, Palmer Higgins. "I figured out why those papers are missing all the time. A kid I know is taking them."

Palmer a law and order man called the Flagler Beach Police who set up their own surveillance.

They too saw Aerial Steward stealing papers. That was the tip of the iceberg.

When they went to the trailer where Aerial and his sister now lived by themselves, they found stolen property. Most had been stolen by the missing father.

Aerial Steward, just turned seventeen, was charged as an adult for several offenses including the most serious thefts performed earlier by his father. He was sentenced to six months in a juvenile facility well away from his home town.

It was during this time that his mother passed and his sister Bailing, was involved in a car crash that left her crippled.

Aerial, the only known relative other than a father who everyone knew was not a responsible adult was released to attend his mother's funeral and care for his sister.

Even the brief time behind bars seemed to harden the boy. He had learned to throw fists in that place. Lying there in his cell he spent his time placing blame for his predicament on others.

They say don't look back but Aerial Steward did just that. He looked back to the night his father had gone missing. The night he confronted his father and hit him with a baseball bat.

When he didn't get the paper carrier job his father began harassing him nightly. This went on for some time. Drunk and abusive the harassment turned physical. Aerial, big and strong and increasingly angry, finally had enough and struck back.

His father with a broken arm and injured knee limped off into the night. He never returned.

Aerial soon after was left holding the bag for his father's crimes. He looked for someone to blame. In the end he blamed, *That damn Wayne Garrett.*

Fresh out of jail Aerial was left to take care of himself and his sister in that little tin can of a place. His sister drove him crazy. Never one to show initiative even before being injured, she now simply issued orders from her bed then her wheel chair.

From sun up till sundown Aerial was forever wheeling the girl from bed to bath to breakfast. The girl ate and ate and ate. When her brother couldn't muster up a meal good enough or fast enough she began harassing him calling him a loser.

Charged and sentenced for his father's crimes, and now seemingly to a life sentence caring for his sister, Aerial rationalized the continued stealing and selling of what he stole.

He continued to see Wayne delivering his papers every morning just like clockwork. To his mind his troubles began when he didn't get that job. For that he continued to blame Wayne Garrett.

From that first brush with the law, and his incarceration to a much later trip to Starke, Florida in the back of a prisoner van, Aerial etched the name Wayne Garrett in his brain. His sister was put in an assisted living facility and she blamed her brother for that.

As for Wayne Garrett, he knew nothing of all this blame.

* * *

Years passed as years tend to do.

Aerial Steward bounced around the state upon his release. He surfed the waters from Miami to Virginia Beach, never remembered in a single community. He worked in bars and cheap fast food restaurants, learned the job of a mechanic, and even took a business course once, never setting foot back in Flagler Beach. He continued to do small time crime and small crime time.

UNTIL. Until, his sister got word to him that she was dying and she sure as shit didn't want to die in a smelly facility.

Word reached him and he came home. He actually spent some time trying to make the place a little more comfortable for his dying sister. She didn't seem to notice and continued to complain twenty four seven. Rolling his eyes as he rolled her to her favorite place, the kitchen table, he secretly began hoping her diagnosis was spot on. He looked over at her, head nearly on the kitchen table, mouth slack but still trying to fill itself. *She shouldn't be buying any green bananas*, he thought. Just like that in a couple of days she was gone.

At the funeral which wasn't really a funeral, the only mourners were people who had cared for his sister over the years.

It was during this trip home he also learned of his father's death years earlier, killed in a bar fight. *Well one bright spot*, he thought.

Aerial who had nothing more than the shirt on his back now took over managing their vast estate; one crumpled trailer complete with all the fixins.

* * *

It was irony maybe, though Aerial would not recognize the word or its meaning if it bit him. It was or fate he'd tell you if asked. He was sitting at the same bench he had ridden years earlier sipping a black coffee just off the Flagler pier when a headline in the News Journal stared up at him. One of those little box things that eats your quarters caught his attention. It was a headline. **Wayne Garrett, Flagler Beach resident saves kid's, life**. He was being touted as a hero.

In a sudden cascading of years, Aerial mustered up a nearly forgotten grievance. His face darkened, his blood boiled, his pulse raced, he began sweating, he nearly passed out. He thought he might be having a heart attack. He sat back and breathed in slowly, the cloud eventually passing from his mind. *Now that was a rush*, he thought.

To a passerby he would have appeared as a fifty-something-year-old- beach bum hanging on to the memories of when he could stand atop a board and defy the gods who attempted to dump him to the bottom of the sea.

When his heart calmed and the sweat on his skin dried it wasn't a surf board that filled Aerial's mind, it was a sudden need for revenge for long ago perceived grievances.

CHAPTER ELEVEN

The Garrett household was discombobulated. Their father was still in rehab, the finances had been compromised, the girls were confused and Becky, well she was just plain pissed. She had to take a leave of absence from her job. With all that was going on there simply wasn't time in the day.

The girls had reverted back to a younger version of themselves and whined about everything. The youngest complained of aches and illness, trying to stay home while hanging on the sleeve of her mother.

The middle child Shellee, had withdrawn further into herself she seemed to be standing outside herself trying to figure this all out.

Marla the oldest was just plain angry. Her senior year was gone to shit and she had no problem expressing that sentiment, promising violence if she came across the creep.

Amidst all this chaos Becky was trying to navigate their insurance situation. Wayne was going to continue to need rehab on an out-patient basis once he was released from in-house therapy; another insurance Rabbit hole.

At every turn Becky felt stymied. Elevator music, long hold times, and then the sound of nothing when the connection was broken filled her days.

Sitting there on the lanai with a phone stuck in her ear she did have time to think.

The letters they had received opened in her mind. Who would do something like this?

Wayne seemed to have no clear idea. Becky had sat with Wayne's supervisor who too seemed in the dark. The one clue, if in fact it was a clue, pointed to something that might have happened a long time ago.

Maybe Wayne's benefactor could help.

Alive, but confined to a wheel chair, 92 year old Mr. Jamie Collins, the very man who had given them this house when he moved to a retirement home years ago, was still (right in the head, his term for his cognitive skills.)

Becky had met Mr. Jamie Collins many times at family celebrations over the years.

Wayne had first introduced her when he proposed marriage. The man asked questions in a peculiar way but in the end blessed their union.

At their wedding a generous gift followed an Irish toast. Wayne had shown Becky the ring Mr. Collins had given him years earlier. One of the questions posed on their first meeting was how would Becky feel about Wayne wearing that ring permanently? The right answer to that question bore fruit when several years later he offered them a permanent home.

Sitting here on the lanai, Becky tried to reconstruct the toast. She could see in her mind's eye the tall handsome man with a mane of silver locks holding a pint aloft and spouting his wishes for the couple. *"Here's to a long life and a merry one. A quick death and an easy one. A pretty girl and an honest one. A cold pint and another one."*

Wayne had shared with Becky the history between Mr. Collins and his mother, who on that day while clearly still in love with the man, sat at the very end of the table three chairs away from the raised glass.

Over the years, on special holidays (including and most especially St. Patrick's Day,) Mr. Collins would be part of the family celebrations. He attended Wayne's mother's funeral but offered no public words.

Wayne for years stopped by weekly to share any news he thought might interest Mr. Collins. The man served as Godfather to all three of the girls. But as the years passed and his girl's grew he spent less and less time with his old benefactor.

Becky felt she needed to draw from the memory of a man who had in one way or another tagged along throughout Wayne's life. She entered the assisted living facility that bordered the Intercoastal waterway a scant half mile from the Atlantic Ocean.

The facility had escaped the flooding from two named storms in 2016 and 2017. First Hurricane Matthew, then just over a year later, Hurricane Irma. Both storms tore up beaches, roadways, homes and businesses, from the inland waterway to famed A1A, to the walkovers along the ocean from one end of Flagler County to the other and beyond. St. Johns and Duvall counties suffered their own misery before the storms made their escape from Florida then rinsed themselves dry in the low country of South Carolina.

A painting of a street of blue tarped roofs done by one of the residents hung above the receptionist desk.

While Becky waited for someone to appear she studied the painting. Memories of hunkering down with her family wondering if their roof would disappear as the howling winds and sheets of rain sounded like a freight train approaching, had the family holding hands and praying silently. A single battery operated lantern showed the concern on the face of their hero, Wayne Garrett, even as he reassured them.

Signed in, she walked the brightly lit corridor to Mr. Collins room.

He was sitting at a window doing a crossword. Becky marveled at the now shriveled man who according to Wayne, seemed to have maintained his mental acumen even as his body shrunk into itself.

She approached him and placed her hands over his eyes from behind. She mustered one of the man's quotes she had heard over the years. "May you live as long as you want, and never want as long as you live."

Jamie Collins sat back in his wheel chair and sighed deeply. He answered with a quote of his own, demonstrating just how sharp he remained. "It's easy to halve the potato where there's love."

Becky, thinking how Mr. Jamie Collins had given well more than half his potatoes to her family squeezed his shoulders and moved around to face him.

"What brings you here on such a fine day Becky Garrett? Surely you're not here asking me to take a swim in the waters deep?" he kidded.

Becky took his hands in hers. She had found over the years that her own sense of humor dovetailed perfectly with Mr. Collins' need to beat around the bush. She had heard Irishman jokes from her husband and this man since they first met. Well today she had a story to tell and it was no joke.

"Mr. Collins," she breathed out, "our family is in trouble and I hope you can help."

All innate humor left Mr. Collins' eyes and he uttered, "Tell me child."

Over the next hour, Becky repeated as close to line by line as she remembered.

Mr. Collins had been made aware of Wayne's accident but that was the limit of what he had been told.

"Do you remember anyone in particular from your long conversations on the porch with Wayne over the years that might shed some light on who could be doing this to our family?"

The hour long one-sided recitation had tired Mr. Collins. He looked into the face of one of the few important people in his life and he gave a final quote that indicated he'd cogitate on all this and get back to her. "In every land lass, hardness is in the north of it, softness in the south, industry in the east and fire and inspiration in the west."

Becky wasn't sure of all the lines but it was clear the message had gotten through to Mr. Collins.

As Becky tucked the old man beneath a light blanket and said her goodbyes his eyes were already closing.

CHAPTER TWELVE

When Jamie Collins returned to Flagler Beach in the spring of 1971 he was forty years old. A clipping of a wedding carried in his wallet assured him there was no one waiting his return.

Yet here he be.

Where had the years gone? College, followed by a successful career in the military filled most of the gap. He had seen the world dressed in its best and worst garb.

As a military officer during Vietnam he had witnessed the idiocy of war, and the simple kindness offered by those who suffered the most.

One thing had been made clear as he was charged with clearing village after village; he never wanted children.

So though promises had been made years earlier, Mr. Jamie Collins had never found his way back to Flagler Beach until he returned for good.

He did make it just south of there once on a three day furlough to Daytona Beach.

When the bus let him off on that single occasion he fully intended to call the girl he knew was waiting in Flagler Beach but fate intervened. He had struck up a conversation on the bus that carried him to the famed racing town. Two strangers in the night moved the conversation from the bus to the bar. The three days that followed passed in a fog of whiskey and pent up passion.

When he left to return to his base three days later, he was thoroughly confused by women in general and now one in particular. Liquor had fueled a release of pent up emotions Jamie mistook for passion and he thought he was in love. Unfortunately the lady involved just wanted a good time. On the morning of the third day he awoke in a room with a note expressing exactly that; **Thanks for a good time, not a long time**.

What he couldn't know was the passion he had released would have a long lasting result.

* * *

Several years later a simple phone call changed his determination to avoid Flagler Beach at all costs. Declan Collins was dead.

Jamie Collins hated his father and was determined to never be in the same room with him again. *Well at least that part had worked out,* he thought.

As he waited for the military paperwork to clear that would allow him to attend the funeral he thought of the man who would soon be under the shovel. So much of his father seemed rooted in the soil in a different place; his father's birth place, Ireland.

During Jamie's time in the armed forces he found his way to Ireland. So much of what his father foisted on him as a kid seemed to have emanated from the Emerald Isle.

Growing up he was told how the family name had royalty attached to it and how he must hold himself to a higher standard because of it. Jamie felt since he had been shaped by a standard that kept him from taking part in the joys of childhood. He needed to know more about this land of limericks and leprechauns; though he never heard that side of Ireland's history from his father.

Declan Collins didn't share humorous Irish stories, or witty limericks with his son. Rather he dwelled on the injustices that he felt had been foisted on the Irish and how only a pursuit of perfection would keep the boy from wasting his days in a pub quaffing Guinness while toasting and quoting some inane reference to a land he knew nothing of.

'Truth be told there is no joy in being Irish, Jamie,' he often said.

So Jamie Collins took an R&R to Ireland. He spent three weeks there. He visited a country that was still at war with itself. A country that in fact for centuries had been at war with itself.

Before heading to the island Jamie read several books covering the geography, history, and culture of Ireland, past and present. By the time he arrived he had a working knowledge of the Country. And it was not lost on him that the Country was informally referred to as the, **Land of Troubles**.

He didn't visit the local pubs. Rather he traveled to each of the four geographic regions mirroring the compass readings of north, east, south, and west.

His plane landed in County Cork along the southern coastline. His mission he decided was to visit the libraries and museums and castles in each of the four regions and come to his own conclusion about his heritage.

He also planned to pursue the origin of the family coat of arms his father gave him in the form of a ring when he left home for college. *'Remember who you are son,'* his father told him. Over time Jamie came to believe the ring was less a gift and more an ever present reminder of just that; *Remember who you are son.*

For three weeks he visited castles, libraries, and museums in all four of the regions of the country. His head spun as he tried to digest the centuries of warfare, religious animosity, persecution, and in the end the hardiness of the common man. It was the common man with dirt under his fingernails, and a near paralytic grip on a Guinness, who turned hate into humor, punishment into parable, and peat bogs into poetry.

When he returned to his military assignment all he had pondered over the last month was made abundantly clear one evening in the barracks. The simple act of a soldier suffering a breakdown while sitting at a table. The man's hands were locked together as if in mortal combat. He mumbled nonsensically to himself, cheering for each arm in turn. A bottle of Ireland's finest whiskey the only visible referee. The entire barracks bore witness.

After calming things down Jamie went back to his room and for the first time in a long time poured himself a tumbler of whiskey he had purchased on his trip. He studied the amber liquid, turning it every which way but loose. In the swirl clarity set in. Jamie made the leap of a simple man wrestling with his demons, to the country where the demons originated. *Ireland too for all of its history seemed to have been trying to pin its own arms.*

* * *

Jamie sat with the family lawyer and was given inventory of all that was now his. A healthy bit of money, a four story tenement building and a two story house, both within hearing distance of the mighty Atlantic Ocean.

He asked the family lawyer to monitor his property however he saw fit and returned to finish his military obligation.

He returned to Flagler Beach nearly four years after that furlough in Daytona Beach.

There were tenants in the four story building and a couple Jamie had known all his life living in and caring for the family home. Jamie was glad not to return to his former residence. The place was too big, and carried to many one sided conversations.

Jamie, not willing to displace his tenants in the apartment building took a two room apartment near the beach and unwound by taking long walks along the water. The only good memories of the town seemed to be when he was near the water. He brought home with him fond memories of just two people; both women. One he had grown up with and shared a promise not kept. The second memory was just a name. The three days in Daytona Beach resurfaced when word reached him that the only girl he'd ever had a physical relationship with was in a jam.

Those years ago the girl had left him with just a cryptic note and her name. Now that name was on his lips and his mind once again.

On a late Saturday morning he climbed the stairs to reintroduce himself and announce to each of his tenants that he was now living on site. All was well on the second and third floor; older couples who seemed solid.

On the fourth floor Jamie Collins met the Steward family. The mother, Isabel, (she of the three days and nights spent in Jamie Collins embrace) immediately averted her eyes and withdrew to the kitchen table.

Jamie recognized her, took a deep breath and introduced himself to Larry Steward. Two youngsters stared out of a darkened bedroom, wide eyed and feral looking.

Larry Steward wore his hair long, bleached white from the sun. His face and arms nearly black, weathered and windblown. The man stuck out his hand in greeting and introduced himself. "Haven't I seen you some place Mr. Collins?"

Looking into a nearly toothless mouth Jamie responded, "I'm sure you have Mr. Steward but you might not remember where. I keep more or less to myself but I do get around."

Larry shrugged off the comment and offered a smile that was more of a grimace. Larry Steward looked nearly normal in the morning light but from what Jamie had observed, when the sun went down and the waves lessened, Larry Steward transformed from the surfer dude he purported to be, into a wild man.

Jamie had witnessed a series of brawls and profanity instigated by the man standing before him. The man had already lost most of his teeth and his smile appeared pasted on.

Jamie alone with not much to do filled his evenings by frequenting the local bars. Not a big drinker he spent his time listening to the local gossip and paying attention to his tenement building.

There was a storm brewing on the fourth floor. A storm that had begun in Daytona years ago was now on his doorstep. This man Larry Steward, his tenant on the fourth floor was outrageous in his actions and profane in his speech. First observed in the local bars lately Jamie was hearing of Larry's actions through the paper thin walls of his building.

What is Larry Steward bringing to the supper table except calamity, wondered, Jamie as he watched the man perform at the pub?

So after hearing of numerous visits by law enforcement to his building when the first floor of his tenement building became vacant, Jamie decided to move in and become an on-site landlord.

Settled back on his first floor porch Jamie felt he had set a tone for conduct that even the dimwitted Larry Steward could understand

Jamie took to his porch nearly every evening, rocking and reading and planning his next day.

You could set your clock to the midnight arrival of Larry Steward. You could check your clock a scant five minutes later and you'd hear the alarm from above go off; a yell or a scream or a swear.

One evening as darkness crowded the porch Isabel sat in a porch rocker on the first floor and filled in some of the gaps of the past four years.

Jamie Collins remained passive but his mind was running rampant.

* * *

Life happened, time passed, and Jamie Collins watched it all from his porch.

Then one night the screams got louder and lasted longer and Jamie Collins climbed the steps that flanked the building.

When he got to the top, he knocked. All went quiet. Ever the gentleman Jamie waited, but didn't leave. He knocked once more and then again.

Finally Larry Steward arrived with a lopsided smile and a mean cut on his brow. Jamie Collins saw the wife Isabel, slumped and bleeding at the table.

Jamie Collins took a deep breath as a quote from his father filled his head.

He looked Larry Steward dead in the eye. "Those who live by the sword get shot by those who don't."

Larry tried to muster a response but was met with a single finger an inch from his face. "I'll be hearing your boot heels descending those stairs a scant half hour from now and I'll not be hearing them return, ever."

Bleary eyed and swaying as if riding a board, Larry Steward decided in the moment the six foot man standing before him wasn't offering up any way to avoid crashing on the rocks.

The door closed and Larry dawdled only briefly. Isabel pointed her own finger and Larry gathered his things. The boy, Aerial had watched it all; the blaring and the beating and now the retreating. The toddler Balin, slept through it all.

* * *

A month later Isabel, her son, named Aerial and toddler Balin, moved out of her own accord. To a better place she envisioned. She had earlier returned to the porch one last time.

Mr. Jamie Collins nodded and offered what he could offer. Isabel refused most of what Mr. Collins offered but did allow the man to help with the security deposit on a small trailer that he arranged for.

* * *

Another storm arose when a different name surfaced. The girl from his hometown (he had grown up and had planned a future with,) was the wife of a very troubled man. The name came from the lips of Roman Garrett himself.

As mentioned earlier Jamie who was mostly a non-drinker still liked the comradery of men. Not a club joiner the local drinking establishments offered a good deal of laughter with little commitment or expense. It was here Jamie Collins first laid eyes on Roman Garrett.

Roman Garrett was like an ocean wave trying to re-shape a beach. He was allowed to land at whatever table he chose but ignored as just another endless lapping of sand and rock.

Communities seem to seek and gravitate to their own roots and the Irish had a strong toe-hold in Flagler Beach.

Roman Garrett for whatever reason had chosen the role of an Irish wannabe. The problem was, first of all he was an Englishman, secondly he couldn't hold his drink, third his tongue, fourth not a thread of useful conversation; and by the numbers if you're counting, fifth of all, he never mastered the self-deprecating humor the Irish use with one another.

Roman Garrett seemed to have a single friend who tolerated him. A man who was as tortured as Roman himself; Larry Steward.

From a distance Jamie watched. *Why aren't you home with that beautiful woman?* Jamie was not much of a drinker but teased a glass and raised it when a celebration was in order.

Larry Steward might be gone from the building but continued his days on the water and nights in the watering holes. Whenever Larry spotted Jamie in the wings he did not make eye contact but rather left immediately for calmer waters to navigate.

When Isabel Steward and her two children moved out, Jamie made contact with and offered the fourth floor flat to Margaret Garrett, the girl he had always called Peg. The terms were more than fair. Roman Garrett was not consulted in the move.

Sitting on his porch Jamie listened to the sounds of the night and sounds from above. From those sounds he felt like he could predict the future for his tenants. He paid special attention to the fourth floor.

He continued to see the little boy, Aerial on his walks to the beach with his mother Isabel and toddler Bailing. He tried to remain positive but it seemed the family was doomed from the beginning.

Larry Steward bounced into the bar one evening announcing the birth of a new daughter hoping that would get him a free glass of ale. 'Here's to my baby daughter, Bailing.' **Though in fact the daughter was nearly three years old at that point.** Larry did manage a pint or two before the audience caught on and the evening ended with fists being thrown.

Larry wasn't completely lying through his teeth. His wife Isabel had stupidly let Larry back into her life and Larry was seeing his kids for the first time in a long time.

Mr. Jamie Collins heard all the ruckus and took a deep breath. He was tied to this family as tightly as the drunken sot pretending to be a new father.

The Steward family, now living in a trailer not that far away from the tenement house remained part of Jamie Collins' world. Jamie found the boy, Aerial shivering on his porch one morning. He offered hot chocolate. The boy barely spoke but Jamie could see the anger he held inside. He welcomed him to come back anytime but Aerial on the rare occasion he did appear seemed distant. While the boy seemed to relax and breathe easier in that chair on the porch he didn't ask for anything beyond a brief respite from his circumstance.

He wanted so to tell the boy the larger story but Isabel had admonished him not to muddy the mind of a boy already struggling. So Jamie simply offered the comfort of a porch rocker whenever he'd like.

Time on a porch was not enough to shape the boy who was being abused at home but would never let on.

As he grew, Aerial began acting out even on his visits. Jamie was patient but admonished him when necessary. Aerial eventually stopped dropping by.

*   *   *

Meanwhile another little boy had been growing day after day year after year on the fourth floor. Jamie Collins grew to love Wayne Garrett as his own. That boy, Wayne, soaked in every word Jamie spoke and when the time was right he would become a businessman with his own paper route. Over time Jamie helped him solve issues ranging from proper payment to countering sabotage of his efforts.

CHAPTER THIRTEEN

Becky settled the financial issues with her bank. The money removed from her checking account could not be recovered. Her savings account provided restitution but the family was still out $3000. Days passed and the family hoped for the best. The best didn't last. The girls were about to be taken for a ride.

Though the deepening Covid crisis seemed intent on adding to everyone's woes, on this particular morning a bus stopped per usual in front of their home. When the girls walked up the steps to enter the bus there appeared to be a new driver aboard. It was hard to tell since everyone wore a mask these days.

The four or five students who were normally aboard when the girls climbed the steps, were not in attendance, which in the days of Covid was not all that unusual. The driver, masked which was becoming a familiar sight, seemed preoccupied and did not face the girls.

When they were seated and the bus was moving, without looking at the girls the driver asked a muffled question? "Do you girls know what today is?"

Marla, Shellee, and Dorothy looked at one another then shrugged, not sure through the muffled mask what was being asked. Marla answered for the group, "Did you ask what day it is Mr. Bus driver?"

The driver wearing a knitted black cap and a surgical mask turned his head. For the first time he made eye contact with the girls. "I did." He paused long enough to draw their interest. "I'll tell you what day it is. Today is 10-10, 20-20. It's your lucky day."

The girls were stymied.

In that moment the driver pulled the bus to the side of the street.

"We're going on a little field trip today girls." He let that statement sit for a moment. "By the way hand me your cell phones."

The girls looked to one another their eyes clouded in confusion. They exchanged looks and frowns and hesitated. The driver rose slightly in his seat, his tone changed. "The phones right now or this gets ugly."

Dorothy was the first to take out her phone and move slowly to the front her hands shaking. She very cautiously handed it over.

"See, your little sister Dorothy is the smart one. Shellee bring both your phone and your sister Marla's, up here, now."

Shellee was the athlete of the family and loved contact sports, she rose up to protest.

Just as she opened her mouth the driver spoke. "I've seen many a surfer wet and soggy hugging the bottom by misjudging the wave, kid. So do as I say."

With the phones collected the bus returned to the roadway. The driver turned south on A1A, the opposite direction of how the girls normally went to school.

The only sounds during what was to be a three mile ride were the normal squeaks of an aging bus and the continual hum of the tires.

When the bus reached the street just north of a water tower three miles from town, the driver turned right. He pulled the bus over to the right hand side of the street where no houses were visible.

The voice from the front became almost buoyant. "Did you catch that I know all your names." Yeah I know a lot about you so listen up."

He stood in the aisle and glared at them. "What we're going to do now is play a little game. Now if you stay calm and answer my questions honestly, maybe you get home in time to get to school after-all"

The girls sat five rows back hugging their jackets, shaking.

An occasional automobile passed the stopped school bus but no one took notice. The day outside the bus was warming nicely. Inside the girls continued to hug their coats and shiver. Shellee was seething inside, already planning an escape for the three of them.

The driver asked his first question. "Which one of you does Wayne love the most?" When they didn't answer he reframed the question, "OK which one of you does your father love the least?"

The girls looked at one another, Dorothy began to speak but Marla told her to hush. "Our father loves us equally."

You could nearly see a smile appear. "Wrong answer. Think about it all of you." He pointed. "Eenie- meanie- miney- moe who would be the first to go." This time he laughed aloud.

"I know for a fact your father treats two of you differently than he does the other. Tell me who that other is and I'll take you back. If not, you will each end up in a separate location today; a long way from home with no money, no phone."

The girls talked quietly among themselves. Finally Marla cleared her throat, "My father likes me the least. I am constantly nagging him for more freedom. And I bug him all the time for a car. It makes him mad."

"You wouldn't be making all this up so I'll let you go would you?" He stood and shouted out to Dorothy, "Dorothy is your sister telling the truth. If you lie I'll know."

Dorothy began to cry, she was really scared. She blubbered, "I don't know Mr. Driver can't you just take us home?"

Shellee folded her younger sister into her arms and glared at the driver.

The driver checked his watch, started the bus, backed up and turned back onto the roadway. The bus began what would be a sweep of a series of Condo buildings.

When the driver reached the last one he turned the bus around and headed back toward A1A. He looked both ways nodding to himself then turned right once again, away from town and further from their home.

Soon they were in Volusia County. A long barren stretch of preserve appeared on the right while the Atlantic Ocean was hidden from view on the left by Palmetto and scrub vegetation.

When a road on the right appeared after several miles, the driver turned right once more.

This area was part of a scenic drive favored by visiting motorcycle operators and Sunday excursionists. A mile or so in, small bogs and streams appeared. The driver found a little used path on the right and pulled the bus in far enough to be invisible to passers-by.

The girls had all moved to the same seat and were hugging one another. When the bus stopped they looked out the window. The girls knew where they were. It was actually a favored Sunday drive for the family. They didn't say a word.

When the driver stood once again to face them they expected the worst. They had all agreed that if he approached them physically, they would all fight and bite to the death.

"So here we are. Any idea what I might have planned for you?"

"We just want to go home. Does this have anything to do with those letters?" asked Marla.

"You might be the least loved but you're the smartest. I'm impressed." He held up his hands. "I'm not going to hurt any of you. At least not this time." He let that sit. "I just want to send a message."

He cleared his throat, "So listen up. The message is, I could have hurt you." He nodded his head, "Tell old Wayne that." That too was followed by silence. "Tell him I could use some of that money he's received over the years from his favorite landlord. If he comes through, this nightmare might just end."

He opened the door and waved his hand dismissively, "Now get out. You are all smart girls so find your way home." He held up one of the phones I'm going to keep these." He snapped his fingers, "Oh by the way give me your passwords on your way out. I may need to be back in touch. Your friends will know how to reach you, right?"

The girls had a lot of things they wished to say but now was not the time. They squeezed by the man who was semi-blocking the aisle. Marla was last, the man patted her behind. Startled, she gasped and leaped from the bus with his laughter following. The girls grabbed one another's hands and disappeared into the foliage. They peeked out just as the bus was disappearing from view.

* * *

Becky, thinking the girls were in school, was enjoying a second cup of coffee. She checked her watch. It was nearly time to get Wayne dressed and out the door to rehab. An hour later she was reading the News Journal while the physical therapist put Wayne through a grueling work out.

It was October 10 according to the paper, her mother's birthday. Her Mom had passed but on this special day Becky always summoned her to mind. With all that had been going on she was glad of the reminder. *Mom what would you think about all this?*

Becky came from a large family. One sister and four brothers all living away from Florida and for the most part out of mind. Calls coming in only when a celebration was called for.

An independent streak ran throughout the family and they cut one another little slack, ribbing each other in most situations. Becky's Mom was the nurturer while her dad brought home the money but exacted re- payment in cruel ways.

Becky shook away her family and tried to focus on the morning headlines. A series of break-ins at Flagler high School had authorities stymied. Little had been taken from the building but it seemed at least one bus was missing. Becky made her way to the comics just as her cell rang.

"Mrs. Garrett? This is the Secretary from the High School. Did your daughter leave for school this morning?"

"Yes of course she did. I saw her heading onto the bus myself and watched it leave. What's going on is she not at school?"

"We are as confused as you are. Several other parents have called us. Their children were not picked up this morning and they contacted the school.

We hadn't heard from you that's why I called. The regular driver was attacked when he left his home this morning. He's at the hospital." She cleared her throat. "You are sure you saw your daughter get on a bus?"

"You are beginning to scare me," answered Becky her voice rising. "Yes I watched all three of my three girls get on a yellow school bus this morning."

Wayne had finished his therapy and was now walking with a cane in Becky's direction. Becky did not want to panic him so she lowered her voice. "I am going to hang up now and call the authorities. If the girls appear at their schools please contact me."

Wayne could read Becky's body language like a book and raised his brow. "What's happening honey?"

Becky took a deep breath and Wayne's hand. This couldn't be avoided. " I think the girls are missing!"

Wayne dialed 911.

The drive back to their home was filled with silence. Both thinking the same thing without verbalizing. A cruiser was in their driveway when they arrived.

Soon seated on the Lanai with a detective and a uniformed officer who identified himself as the police chief, Wayne sketched what had befallen the family recently.

Wayne nodded to his wife and spoke. "We believe our daughters are being targeted. Do you know anything about their regular bus driver and how this could be connected?"

Detective Jose Estevez who was hearing the whole story for the first time remained skeptical but he did have a report of a missing bus from the fleet at the Flagler bus garage.

"The Sheriff's office is trying to track that bus down but no one has found it as of yet. Might be a connection might not. Right now give me a description of your daughters. Hopefully they are all together."

At that moment Becky's cell rang. She did not recognize the number. She answered anyway. It was a call from daughter, Marla.

"Mom! Mom! Mom, listen! First off, we're ok." Marla took a deep breath and continued, her mother had stopped interrupting. "I am calling from a house in South Flagler Beach."

She told her mother they had been picked up on A1A heading north by an old couple after being released from the bus by a creep.

Her mother could hear Marla asking someone a question. Then the girl's voice continued, "We are at 47 Water View Street in South Flagler Beach."

Becky's heart was in her mouth. She reached for Wayne's hand and announced the girls were ok and they were safe.

The detective and the police chief sat up straight. "Have your daughter give you the address and we'll bring them home. We'll sort all this out," said the detective.

An hour later the three sisters served as centerpieces on that same lanai where a conversation that included Wayne, Becky, the Detective, and the uniformed chief of police for Flagler Beach, Dennis Cusack, was taking place.

Everything that had transpired this morning was repeated, followed up with questions and clarifications. There was an All-points Bulletin out for the missing bus.

One thing the girls could not agree on was a description of the man who had kidnapped and terrorized them. He was tall, he seemed short, he seemed young; he appeared old; he seemed calm; he was agitated.

The one clear message that ruled the day was that the man intended to scare the girls and scare their parents. Wayne and Becky got that message loud and clear.

Wayne spoke up. "Now do you believe that my accident was no accident? That our finances being compromised was no accident? You have read the letters. Our family is under attack."

The detective and police chief listened and had to agree. Someone had the Garrett family in their sights.

In all the excitement the girls forgot about the message they were to deliver. That message of a cash payment would have to come later; by mail.

* * *

In the days following, the bus, burned out, was found. The driver was not.

* * *

A solid month went by with no further incidents. Wayne had ditched the cane and was preparing to go back to work. Becky had returned to her job. The girls had new cell phones equipped with added layers of security.

Marla now had a car and drove herself and her sisters directly to school and home every day.

Slowly smiles replaced the worry lines that had circled the table at dinner time. Wayne remained vigilant and watchful and worried however. Nightly in their bedroom the parents whispered, wondering when the next shoe might drop.

The Flagler police department conducted an increased number of drives through the neighborhood but they still had no suspects.

The Sheriff's office continued to investigate the stolen bus but made no progress.

Wayne rose from his bed and looked out into the darkness. Speaking to his reflection as well as Becky he nodded. "I think it's time to go back and visit Mr. Collins. He's had time to think. Maybe he remembered something. I'm sure he would like to know I'm healing."

CHAPTER FOURTEEN

Steve Hart moved to Flagler Beach in 2016. Arriving from the frozen north where he had spent the first thirty-six years of his life he could not believe his good fortune. An uncle, also named Steve had become ill and Steve the nephew was the only member of his family not attached to someone else.

When the call came his father asked Steve to go south and take care of his brother. "He just needs someone to live with him and do basic stuff. You can still work your profession. Might be a good change for you."

Steve had to admit he had no physical or emotional attachments to anyone. He also had to admit he wasn't loving the cold either.

As a residential plumber, winter was always a challenge. Crawling around under somebody's year-round camp, thawing out pipes after shoveling his way through snow and ice then working his way through spider-webs and debris only to find the problem was going to require more than one trip in and out, left him breathless.

In addition, his hands had begun to pain him from the constant twisting and turning loosening and tightening; freezing cold magnified all that.

So in the fall of 2016 he arrived at his Uncle Steve's house in Flagler Beach and became caregiver. His uncle had money so Steve, who was named after his father's brother, provided support and companionship and was well paid for his effort.

To keep himself busy when he wasn't needed, Steve decided he didn't want to continue a career in plumbing down here. Just getting licensed would be a hassle. So he took a job as a twenty hour a week bartender in the evenings at a local bar named, <u>FISH OR CUT BAIT</u>.

Over the next four years during the day he watched his uncle waste away. At night he watched people simply get wasted.

He finally had to place his uncle in a retirement home. Uncle Steve needed twenty-four-seven care now, but remained alert and was quite the hit in his custom designed wheel chair, a replica of the late great Dale Earnhardt's racing machine, complete with the number 3 on the back. His uncle was forever telling stories to the other residents.

In one he told of being there the day the NO. 3 car crashed and killed his idol. He was an encyclopedia of knowledge when it came to Dale Earnhardt. He also regaled with stories of his youth when he surfed up and down the eastern coast of Florida.

A big smile crossed his face as he told of (many young lovelies) following the surf.

When Steve had first arrived his uncle asked to visit the beach for early morning breakfast at the pier. He heard more of his uncle's stories every time they sat down to eat.

Steve was now living in the south where racing holds a life all its own. He took all this information in and filed it away.

Standing there in the dim light polishing glasses while offering up pretzels and feigned sympathy for the hundreds of plights expressed nightly, he could if needed defend the legacy of Dale Earnhardt at all levels.

When Steve took the job of bartender he had no way of knowing the role he would play in the drama of a family he had yet to meet

* * *

When a man who had seen better days because of his nights began to frequent the bar, Steve simply served him with a nod. When the man became a regular, greetings were exchanged, bowls of pretzels offered and conversation that at first remained light.

It didn't take long to learn the man's name, Aerial Steward. It took a little longer to learn his game. Alcohol has a way of loosening a tongue as successfully as a pipe wrench loosens a frozen bolt.

This man, Aerial, was a former surfer dude or so he told Steve. His sister had died recently and so he was now back in his old hometown living in the old homestead so he told Steve the bartender.

Steve was a good listener and his eyesight was twenty-twenty. He could see the jailhouse tats that lined the man's arms. I *guess he didn't spend his whole life on the water,* observed Steve.

In time in casual conversation it came out that Steve used to be a plumber. Steve would later regret mentioning it.

One evening Aerial lamented the problems he was having with leaky faucets and a shower that wouldn't drain. Steve wise cracked, "I think there's an APP for that."

Aerial didn't laugh and didn't seem to know what an APP was.

Steve was about to explain but in the moment seeing the blank look in the man's eyes he simply told Aerial he used to be a plumber.

When Aerial perked up Steve sighed, "I would be glad to take a look at your pipes. "I can't promise I'll fix them but I can at least give you an idea of what it will cost to fix the problem."

So the next day at One o'clock Steve pulled into the driveway of a broken down rusted out trailer. Sitting on the third step in a pair of dirty underpants with his head in his hands was Aerial Steward. He didn't raise his head. The man and the trailer seemed to be in a similar condition.

Steve's first thought was to back right out of the yard and mosey on down the road. He actually put the car into reverse but then his better angel grabbed the wheel. He pulled in and turned off the motor. Aerial had not moved.

Steve looked at himself in the rearview and sighed. He opened the car door and lumbered his six foot two self onto a grown over patch of gravel. He looked at the bright blue sky and felt the warmth of the day and remembered what he would be facing had he remained in the frozen north; things didn't look quite so bleak after all. He approached the steps calling out Aerial's name so as not to jump him.

Aerial came around and looked blankly at Steve. No recollection of what the two had discussed last night entered his eyes.

Steve reminded him that he was here to check out all those leaks he was having.

The light came on and Aerial rose and stretched and moaned aloud. The screen door hanging on one hinge, itself pleading to be put out of its misery, squawked in a manner WD-Forty couldn't touch.

Steve followed him inside where the heat of the day had baked all the dead smells within to a stench that filled the kitchen.

"Can I get you a beer?" offered Aerial as he moved to the fridge, snatched one, opened and began to drain it.

Steve never took a drink when he had work to do. He shook his head, and tried to hold his breath. "Maybe later," he managed, breathing through his nose. "Why don't you show me what's leaking."

Aerial was in the process of swallowing the can of PBR. He finished, burped, and crushed the can throwing it in the direction of an over flowing garbage can. "Just let me get my pants on."

As Aerial wandered to the other end of the trailer (not a very long walk if we're being real) Steve looked around the room. Dirty dishes and greasy paper wrappings dominated every surface. Rust and water spots dotted the ceiling and ran along the tops of curtain-less windows. No pictures, or wall decorations, not even a wall clock. There were however at least a dozen coils of sticky fly paper, with dozens of residents along for the ride, hanging from the ceiling.

On the fridge several newspaper articles attached with magnets were on display. Steve moved closer.

The first was an article with a headline. "Local Hero."

Another reported on a postal worker who had been injured when his postal van crossed a street and struck a house. Steve remembered that article from a while back.

A more recent article about a stolen bus that had been used to briefly kidnap and terrorize three sisters consumed three paragraphs. No one had been hurt but the driver of that bus had not been found.

Steve remembered that story well. That incident had spent a good number of evenings circling the bar. An opinion offered from every bar stool.

Steve didn't have time to ponder further as Aerial hollered for him to come down and check the leaks in the bathroom.

Four hours later Steve had identified the problem, gone to Ace Hardware purchased the materials needed and fixed all the leaks. He made it to the steps and was enjoying that beer.

"What do I owe you?"

"You paid for the PVC and the glue. You don't owe me nothing, I'm not even licensed down here. This beer is enough."

"Well thank you Dude. If people had been just a little nicer back when I was living in this place as a a kid..." He didn't finish, just raised his can.

Steve was about to respond when Aerial added, "Too late now. Now I'm in it to win it."

"What does that mean?" asked Steve.

"Oh nothing, just planning to ditch this tin can in the foreseeable future."

"Well good luck with that." Steve rose, "I need to be going. Got to check on my Uncle in the nursing home."

* * *

An hour later Steve was at the nursing home spoon feeding an early supper into his Uncle. Uncle Steve was slowly dying but from the quickness of his mind you would never know it.

"So what did you do with your day Bub, something fun I hope?" He chewed then swallowed the broccoli with the same look of disgust his mother had admonished him for decades earlier.

Steve laughed right out loud.

Uncle Steve ignored him. "Did you get to the beach?"

Steve looked with fondness at the man he had been named after. "Well Uncle Steve, kinda sorta. What I did was get wet putting some of my plumbing skills to work in an old trailer in that park on South Flagler Avenue a couple blocks from the water.

His uncle rubbed his chin. "I know that trailer park. Hell I used to own a couple of trailers in there."

"Well I bet you kept your units in better condition than the one I worked on today."

Uncle Steve rubbed his forehead lost in thought. "Knew a family in there actually. First met the father back when he was a one hit wonder on a surf board. He had a trailer right near one I owned." And so began one of his uncle's stories.

"The man sat on the top step of his trailer most every day waxing that board between beers and hollering at his wife and kids." He thought a minute. "Name was Larry Steward. He was rude, crude and fully tattooed." He chuckled aloud, "named his kids after some idiotic surfer talk as I remember."

Steve who had only been half listening perked up. "The guy I did work for today has a weird name, Aerial. When I looked at him funny when he first told me his name he just shook his head. Said his old man named him that."

"Yep, that's got to be Larry's son. I can understand why he referred to him as the 'old man' he was never much of a father as I saw it." Uncle Steve seemed to be reaching back in his mind, then continued. "The useless jerk left the area when the kids were still young and in school. Not sure of the sequence of events but the mother died suddenly the girl got injured and crippled as I recall.

The mother seemed nice though, the couple of times I saw her hanging out clothes when I went to collect from my renters. She kept her kids in clean clothes I'll say that for her." The old man's eyes glazed over. "I think the mother was dead and gone by the time the girl got hurt. During all the leaving and dying and getting hurt the boy got in some kind of trouble and I never heard his name again."

"Well he's back. Probably in the same trailer you remember. He's a drunk and frequents the place I work. His place is a mess."

"Yep it was back then too." Uncle Steve nodded his head and closed his eyes.

Steve could see that this conversation was over. "Well I guess I better get to work. I'll stop in tomorrow."

Steve's uncle picked up his head. "Well bring my clippers with you when you come. I need my ears lowered."

Steve laughed, "You don't mean your hedge clippers do you? Just kidding, I'll see you tomorrow."

* * *

Half way through his shift Steve watched Aerial Steward enter the bar. The way he was weaving indicated he'd made a stop or two before hitting <u>FISH OR CUT BAIT.</u> He made his way to the bar, sat heavily and made eye contact with Steve. He was dressed in cut-off jeans and a stained off white t-shirt that at one time probably bore a message that had long since faded to obscurity.

"PBR," he announced as a way of greeting.

Steve opened the bottle and brought him a glass. He could smell the man's unwashed body from across the bar.

"Save yourself some dishwashing," he piped, "I don't need a glass," his words already slurring. "Thanks again for fixing my pipes." He held up his bottle in a toast.

Steve studied him for a moment. *Dirty face and hair, grimy shirt, a ship wreck on dry land. I fixed your shower maybe you should use it.*

It was a quiet night in Flagler, Monday nights were generally slow with a number of businesses closed on Mondays. Steve thought maybe weekends tired everyone one out.

Aerial, well lubricated seemed eager to talk so Steve listened.

Foul language embraced at least one of the eight parts of speech in nearly every sentence. Aerial in this state of inebriation seemed to be missing his little sister. His eyes got wet. He blubbered. Finally he Shook off the memory and added with a scoff, "She never was little as I remember."

Steve listened.

Aerial told of being a pretty damn good surfer back in the day. He toasted himself, studying the amber liquid.

Steve listened.

Aerial slurred through stories from his jail house days, amplifying them by pointing to his tattoos.

Steve worked the bar but as quiet as it was on this Monday night eventually made his way back to what seemed a long running commentary.

Finally when Aerial had finished his life story that at each downturn was blamed on someone else, he paused and ordered one for the road. Four dead soldiers stood side by side in front of him.

When Steve tried to remove the empties with the delivery of each new beer, Aerial had held up his hand. "I like to keep count. Just like I keep count of people who have screwed me over."

Steve commented. "Well I haven't screwed you over have I?"

Aerial raised his nearly empty bottle, "Nope you didn't Steve and I thank you for that. Others have though and I'm still giving payback."

"I find holding a grudge just gets in the way," offered Steve.

"Maybe so. Maybe so." He wobbled on the stool. "Too late now though, bills already in the mail." Aerial snickered at what had to be a private joke. He got up and wandered away.

"Well I don't think it's ever too late to do the right thing, my friend. "You take care Aerial."

CHAPTER FIFTEEN

A week passed. Things remained quiet in the Garrett household. No suspects emerged in the kidnapping incident.

Flagler Beach Police Chief Dennis Cusack, was sitting in the Funky Pelican having coffee with his detective and the Flagler County Sheriff, reviewing what they knew, what they didn't know, and planning strategy on how to move forward.

There was no turf war of who was in charge, both were pissed that something like this could happen in Flagler County.

By the time their second cup of coffee had disappeared the trio had made plans to reach out to the public in a very public way.

They agreed to meet right back here the next morning and put their plan into action.

Bright and early the next morning their action plan joined them at their table. The sun was up and a calm breeze coming off the water offered a positive spin to what they intended to do.

The three officers and two reporters, one from the Palm Coast Observer and the other from the News Journal, moved their meeting to the deck looking out over the mighty Atlantic Ocean. Little sea birds landed on the railing begging for a scoop of their own. After introductions and small talk about the weather and how lucky they all were to live in Florida, they got down to business.

The idea was spelled out to the reporters on a small portable white board. Ideas were thrown about, dismissed, or added to. What emerged was a plea to the public to read a comprehensive timeline of what the Garrett family had faced, and see if you the reader might have information on any part of it.

The Flagler Beach police chief took the lead this morning. "Frame your story anyway you want, get graphic about what these girls experienced. Make the readers sit up and take notice. We are convinced somebody saw something."

Within the week articles appearing in both publications introduced the public to the human side of the kidnappings. The journalists had reached out to the Garrett family and were allowed to interview the girls with both parents in attendance.

The story that emerged painted a picture of a family being stalked and violated physically mentally and emotionally. The story grew legs and was discussed in salons and saloons. Everybody had a theory.

* * *

Steve was hearing the rehash nightly in the bar where he worked. He didn't think much about it. He just listened.

* * *

Two weeks after the latest story of the girls' kidnapping had appeared in print, Aerial Steward made his way to the FISH OR CUT BAIT. He had a problem. His trailer had sprung another leak. "It's my toilet this time."

Steve wondered in his mind, *in that place how could you tell.* Steve sighed and agreed to take a look.

The next afternoon when Steve arrived to take that look, Aerial provided a de-ja-vu moment.

The man was sitting in the same spot, probably in the same grungy underwear, perched precariously, head hung down. He never moved his head. Aerial's yellowed underwear, his only covering, bagged around a shrunken pair of legs.

Steve sat in his car not willing to move until Aerial moved at least a part of his body. A sure signal the man was alive at least.

Steve tooted his horn lightly.

After seconds passed Aerial finally with great effort raised his head and made eye contact. Seconds more passed as Aerial tried to focus. When he seemed to have his bearings, he rose and turned to the door.

Steve shook his head at the mess of a man facing him, wondering if the man ever bothered to wash. He took a deep breath left his car and followed the mess into the mess that was always a mess..

In the dim kitchen with no light on Aerial nearly disappeared from view. He suddenly announced he needed to get his pants on. "Get yourself a beer if you want?"

Steve remained in what passed for a kitchen. The little bit of light coming in from the still open door highlighted unwashed pans and dishes lining the side board. The sink seemed ready to vomit a belly full of dirty dishes.

Steve walked to a window the blinds were closed. He opened the blind and cranked open the window and sucked in big gulps of fresh air.

He turned and the new light showed the refrigerator that seemed to have new articles attached. In the light from the open window Steve read the headlines.

Two recent articles, the ones he heard discussed nightly at the bar, were taped over older articles Steve had scanned previously.

Steve wondered to himself why Aerial Steward was so interested in all this that he had posted the articles. Aerial returned at that moment opened the refrigerator and grabbed a couple beers. "C'mon I'll show you where it's leaking."

CHAPTER SIXTEEN

Wayne was getting stronger by the day. He was just leaving a doctor's appointment that cleared him to return to work. He breathed in fresh air that held no humidity. He was feeling thankful.

Sitting in his car he began counting his blessings. Christmas was fast approaching and the last few weeks had been uneventful. Kids are resilient and smiles and teasing had returned to the house.

Wayne who throughout his life had taken the high road began to think maybe the worst was over. He had just turned on the radio to a favorite station ready to hum or whistle along when his cell phone rang. It was wife Becky.

"Somebody trashed my car. Both taillights are broken and all four doors have been dented!"

Wayne took a deep breath. The air didn't seem so fresh and invigorating about now. Christmas seemed a long ways away and all that came in on his station was a commercial advertising a great deal on the latest model Toyota.

Becky continued, "I was parked where I always park," her voice was shrill. "When Lucy showed up for her shift she asked me what had happened to my car." Becky began crying, her voice nearly broken, "This is more of the same isn't it?"

Wayne could feel the helplessness in his wife's voice, he felt nauseous. He sucked it up, "Do you want me to come get you? Have you called the police? I'll be there in ten minutes."

"Hurry Wayne, I'm scared."

Wayne entered route 100 at Belle Terre and turned left. New businesses stood on his right; a Starbucks, Tractor Supply, Taco Bell, anchored by an Aldi's food store indicated the city of Palm Coast continued to grow. Wayne saw none of them as his mind raced, *his family was still under attack.*

Minutes later as he sped the bridge over the Intercoastal, he failed to slow as he descended to enter Flagler Beach. A sudden siren, and when he checked his mirror, flashing lights added to the despair he was feeling. He pulled into the first side street available and waited for the officer to exit his police vehicle the anger welling up inside him.

The officer was courteous and professional. He even smiled as he asked to see Wayne's license and registration. Wayne couldn't hide his fury which the officer misinterpreted as directed at him.

Wayne was asked to exit his vehicle and place his hands on the roof of his car. Another patrol car pulled up and after the two officers conversed, Wayne was handcuffed and placed in the back of the patrol car. He hung his head.

Meanwhile Becky waited.

Two hours later Wayne showed up at Becky's place of work.

Wayne had managed to get the attention of Flagler Beach Police Chief Dennis Cusack who recognized him immediately.

After a cordial discussion it was agreed the fine for speeding would stick but Wayne would not be charged with disrespecting and resisting an officer in the performance of his duties.

Wayne was shaken by all of it. Two hours in custody sitting by himself in a small cell with no windows gave him time to think. The holding cell smelled of recent visitors who needed a good shower. Between holding his breath and breathing through his teeth, while trying to figure out this mess, Wayne sat with his head in his hands. Thank God the chief came in this morning and immediately recognized his name.

When he finally showed up at Becky's work place, Roger's Towing was already loading Becky's vehicle onto a flat-bed taking it to a repair shop. Wayne and Becky watched from a distance as they compared notes.

"This is all too crazy to be real. What will we tell the girls? They are just beginning to get their lives back on track." Becky's voice rose like a rogue wave hitting the beach. For the first time in their marriage Wayne didn't seem to have any answers. He hung his head and teared up.

"I am so sorry if this is all because of something I did or something I said, I just don't have any answers."

Becky took his hand. She realized her reaction to the damage done to her car had not been helpful. They were a team. They needed to be strong for one another. "Let's get that cup of coffee we've been missing for a while and go look for answers in the waves."

* * *

Meanwhile, Aerial was back on the top step at his trailer toasting himself on a job well done. *Maybe that will get their attention.* Either the girls hadn't delivered the message or Wayne wasn't listening. He fully intended to ask Wayne, indirectly (through the mail obviously) to get him $20,000 and this would all end. He had one more card to play first though that should seal the deal. One more little caper that would show the man he was dead serious.

The mid-morning sun promised another good day in paradise. He breathed in fresh air but the recent taste and smell of alcohol and cigarettes dominated what reached his lungs. He hacked aloud, rose and entered his trailer, moving to a cluttered table where a brochure of the schools in Palm Coast was dog-eared on the page that highlighted the High School.

* * *

When the girls got home from school Wayne and Becky chose not to tell them about the vandalism, simply saying Becky's car had broken down and was being repaired. Becky told the girls she would need their transportation for the near future and would take the girls to school and pick them up or they could ride the bus.

The girls hemmed and hawed but in the end thought taking the bus would be easier. The oldest, Marla, spoke up. "If any of us have to stay after school you can come and pick us up."

Becky sighed in relief. Transporting the girls daily would have been a scheduling nightmare. "You girls have been real troopers in all this."

* * *

Night follows daytime and on this night, just like clockwork, Aerial occupied the same stool in the same bar talking to his favorite plumber/bartender.

Steve noticed Aerial seemed particularly upbeat this evening. Nearly sober. Aerial's mouth displayed a seldom seen grin? He was buoyant, his body moving to the music on the jukebox. "Did you meet a lady or come into money?"

Aerial raised his glass. "Small victories man, just small victories. By the way you can soon rent out this stool."

Steve raise his brow quizzically.

Aerial remained mysterious. "Let's just say I'm resuming my education and leave it at that." Aerial checked his watch. "As a matter of fact I should get going."

Steve watched this strange man making an early exit. He was walking straighter. He had consumed a single beer. Steve had learned to take the measure of a man and to his mind this man was not capable of making long term change. He'd be back. *I wonder what he's up to.*

A call for alcohol interrupted pursuit of that thought.

* * *

Aerial, after a rare good night's sleep, was up and out the door while the stars still dominated the early morning sky. He remembered the hundreds of times he had followed the big dipper or some such configuration of stars down to the water's edge and caught the morning sun from the top of a board. Those were the only fond memories of the twenty four hours that constitute a day. Once off the board the real world emerged and it had all been a piece of shit.

"But anyway, let's get to it," he said aloud. Aerial had no car, in fact, he had no license. But he did have an ancient ten speed he'd swiped from an open garage a while back.

Hell the owner probably didn't even know it was missing. Every retiree in Florida had a bike. Most of them showed little wear. Well he was going to put his transportation to good use.

He pedaled furiously up and over the Intercoastal his breath catching with the exertion. The only real hills in this part of Florida were these nearly half mile long spans over the Intercoastal. When he reached the highest point he stopped to regain his breath. He looked down at the long line of blackness and not a single thought reached his mind. After leaving the bridge he rode a three mile stretch of route 100 and turned right. Aerial Steward had arrived at his destination.

Today would mark the first shift for Aerial Steward as a janitor at Palm Coast High School.

CHAPTER SEVENTEEN

Wayne knocked on the door. After a second knock Jamie Collins bade him enter. The single room in the assisted living facility was laid out with a bed, a recliner with a small table housing a lamp, a chair, and a bureau with a forty inch TV. A bathroom door and closet door stood closed.

Light from a single window with blinds partly open kept the room dim. Mr. Jamie Collins was sitting back in his recliner with a newspaper draped over his lap. *Probably he'd been dozing*, thought Wayne.

A hand shake and an invitation to 'rest your bones' brought Wayne face to face with his aged friend and mentor.

"It's good to see you up and around my boy. Have you started back to work yet?"

"Not yet. I have a lot on my plate right now if I'm being honest."

"So I read." Uncle Jamie threw out an Irish proverb. "The dark holds sway only for a time."

"Well it appears it's still about midnight in our household, so I could use your help. Have you come up with who could be behind this?"

Jamie Collins, shook his head. "I have witnessed evil in many forms over the years, from the stories told in history books to bearing personal witness on the battlefield."

He looked directly into Wayne's eyes. "This is an evil I have not faced before. I have no insight Wayne, but this seems like a personal test you're facing."

"It's as personal as it can get and I have no idea why or who is behind it."

"How can I help?"

CHAPTER EIGHTEEN

"There's not a whole hell of a lot to do during this shift. We pretty much wait for the shit to hit the fan then we respond," announced Aerial's co-worker.

The two men were in the doorway of the janitor's supply closet. Behind them shelves filled with cleaning supplies, toilet paper and paper towels lined the walls. Electric floor cleaning machines used during the late afternoon and overnight were lined up like race cars ready to do battle.

A bell rang and students entered what had been a deserted corridor. Aerial and his co-worker remained invisible to the throng of yapping teens finding their lockers, dumping books, exchanging high fives and hugs; all the while they moved like herded cattle to their next class.

Mouths moved, noise bounced off the lockers, bodies sent out messages ranging from bullying, to teasing, to love, to hate and every emotion in between.

As Aerial watched one kid get tripped and his books scattered to the four winds, he nodded to himself remembering those days when he and his sister were singled out for who they were and what they came from. His mother, keeping her kids clean and patched, had not been enough to keep the jackals at bay.

Aerial Steward had spent just a brief time in halls like these. Most of his education had come from the Ying and Yang of his father's closed hands, the fights in the schoolyard, and the uncaring attitude of too many of his teachers. His days on the water helped tamp down his anger but never squelched it. The kindness in his mother's touch was not enough to see him through each day. When he entered the correctional system, a whole new learning experience provided the finishing touches to his view of the world

A second bell rang and it brought quiet back to the corridor. His co-worker spoke, "Now we walk all the corridors and check the bathrooms for any damage these shits have done in the past three minutes."

During the first two class changes Aerial had not spotted Marla Garrett. During the lunch break though, he saw her with a group of boys and girls at a cafeteria table. She seemed at ease.

Probably forgotten all about that bus ride by now, thought Aerial. The two janitors walked casually among the tables with their brooms at the ready. When Aerial spotted a napkin and a stray french-fry near Marla's table he beat feet to get there to sweep them into a dust pan on a stick.

Marla looked up and nodded her thanks. Their eyes met but Marla clearly did not recognize her former captor. Aerial nodded back, smiled and moved on.

Two more afternoon classes passed in a repeat of the morning.

When the dismissal bell rang Aerial placed himself near the exit in an effort to watch the school empty. Sure enough here came Marla, talking excitedly with friends.

When she left the building Aerial thought the day had ended for her. He was still standing there ruminating on nothing really when suddenly Marla walked right past him. Aerial watched the girl walk the length of the corridor and turn right into the gymnasium.

Hmm, I guess our little play date hasn't ended just yet.

Aerial went about his business cleaning up the corridors. The night crew would come on at 4pm. And those cleaning and polishing machines would toe the starting line.

Aerial checked the time 3:38 pm. He looked around, his shift was about done. He wandered to the glass doors of the gymnasium and saw that the bleachers had been pulled back and the gym was halved into two volley ball courts.

Two volleyball nets sitting side by side had girls in shorts and t-shirts standing on both sides of the net trying to drive a volley ball down one another's throats. An occasional whistle accompanied screams and yells and grunts.

Marla Garrett was right in the middle of all this. Tunnel vision allowed Aerial to separate her from the masses. She was a pretty girl he decided. Not too tall. Not too short. Just right, as Goldilocks would say. Aerial chuckled to himself.

He filed all he was seeing away for further pondering even as a plan was forming in his head.

Aerial wandered down to the janitor's closet and greeted the evening shift. He nodded, punched out then stopped in the main office on his way out. He asked a secretary for a winter sports schedule.

His head was filled with possibilities as he climbed the long incline separating land from water. His mind raced his bicycle. Bent over from exertion he hacked up what felt like a pint of phlegm. The ride down the quarter mile decline allowed a rush of air to enter his lungs freeing up even more phlegm. He seemed to be bringing up parts of his lungs as a long continuous hacking wracked his body. He entered his trailer and grabbed a beer.

He attached the sports schedule to the refrigerator even as he removed all the previous articles from their magnets and tossed them into the trash. He looked once again at the Volleyball schedule. He had six weeks to end this, sooner if waves broke his way.

On the way home he had put together a scheme that might be the ultimate payback. He chuckled to himself, *this would be payback that would last a lifetime.* He also composed a letter he needed to get in the Garrett mail box.

He took a nap, woke and checked his watch. It was nearly six-thirty pm. He didn't have a working TV so there was no point in just sitting here. He put on a heavy jacket and walked to the beach. It was near dark now. The wind was coming off the water. Winter had arrived in Flagler Beach. He bought a sandwich then walked back across A1A and stood on the boardwalk facing the mighty Atlantic.

Any good times he had spent here in his youth disappeared in the coming on of night. He had been able to find ways to hide during most days if he wasn't in school. But he couldn't hide from the night.

The closed fist and the beatings at night time arrived in his head as each wave crested and crashed. He chewed on his grievances harder than he chewed on the stale sub from the grocery across the street. He could hate his old man but there was no way to gain revenge on that score.

It would take a normal person great effort to identify a single person or event from the past as the source for their present state of mind but Aerial managed. Once more a name entered his head. *Wayne Garrett this is all on you.* Aerial Steward who had sworn to cut back on his drinking (just as Steve the bartender had predicted) made his way to the <u>FISH OR CUT BAIT</u>.

Dan Fogleberg's, <u>Leader of the Band </u>was playing on the juke box. Behind the counter Steve the bartender was singing along under his breath. *Man that guy can write and sing a lyric*, thought Steve. He had his back turned to the bar and didn't see Aerial reach his destination.

Aerial had not been in for several days and to be honest Steve hadn't missed him. When Steve turned, Aerial, as if by magic, was just sitting there.

"I started a job today Steve, aren't you proud of me?" Aerial opened his mouth in a big smile that would make a dentist cringe.

In the moment, in that mouth Steve saw the outside and inside of that trailer mimicking the rot visible in front of him. He actually shuddered. Aerial noticed. "You cold man, you're shivering."

Ignoring the comment Steve said, "Tell me about this job while I crack you a beer."

Aerial air brushed his day and his responsibilities, then focused on the student population. "Man they don't make those girls like I remember them, take a man's breath away."

"Well I don't recommend you look too close or more than your breath may be taken away."

Aerial raised his bottle, shrugged, "True that, just talking's all."

Steve attempted to change the subject. "So how are my repairs holding up? Spring any more leaks?"

"Funny you should mention that." Aerial stretched, "I'm thinking I need to get rid of that place. Now that I'm working I can do better." He smiled a big open mouth smile and continued, "Gonna get my teeth fixed too."

* * *

The letter arrived in the Garrett household in a very odd way. It had been found taped to the locker of oldest daughter, Marla, when she went to gather her books after Volleyball practice.

The letter was addressed to her father so she did not open it until she got home. Even before Wayne opened the letter a clear message had been re-enforced: *My kids are being used to threaten me.* Wayne held his breath as he tore the letter open. The words got right to the point.

> 50,000 dollars and all this goes away. I was originally thinking 20,000 would do it but you have ignored me. You have two weeks. In one week you will be told where and how to deliver the money. I guess your daughters must have forgotten to give you this message after their little bus trip. Well, I'm telling you now.

"What does it say dad?"

Wayne looked at his daughter, Dorothy, then he addressed, Marla. "This was taped on your locker? And you say it wasn't there when school ended when you went to practice?"

Marla shook her head. Then Wayne read the letter aloud.

Marla sighed aloud and nodded. "Should we tell the school Principal?"

Becky Garrett spoke. "From the letter it sounds like he gave you a message to deliver when he had you on that school bus. Do you recall what he said?"

The three girls looked to one another then tried to piece together what in a kid's world was a lifetime ago. What emerged was something to do with their dad getting help from someone who had helped him in the past.

Wayne knew in the moment who that someone was. But who else knew that? Jamie Collins had never advertised the gifts he had bestowed upon Wayne and his family. It seemed another trip to the retirement home was in order.

The trip was undertaken and two heads tried to unravel the mystery. The conversation ended with Jamie Collins telling Wayne that with this new information he needed to ruminate all this with a different mindset.

* * *

As fate would have it though, just as a breakthrough in this struggle mirrored peace talks between the north and the south of his native Ireland, talks broke down.

CHAPTER NINETEEN

A week passed. Aerial sealed a new envelope. He attached it to the fridge and sat back and lit a cigarette. He removed the athletic schedule from the fridge and studied it. He needed Wayne to know how seriously he should be taking all this.

There was a home volleyball game tomorrow evening. Marla Garrett was on that team, though not a starter.

Aerial had watched a number of practices and knowing the girl wouldn't be starting in the game was critical to his plan.

She wouldn't be immediately missed. Her absence wouldn't send the coach and team into a frenzy.

At five pm Aerial entered the corridor that had been cleaned and abandoned. The silent echoes of a school day were still attached to the walls. The corridor was dimly lit, shadows formed on the highly polished floor as Aerial found Marla's locker. He attached the letter then found a hiding place in the janitor's closet. This end of the building had been thoroughly cleaned and put to bed for the night.

At five thirty he saw through a crack in the doorway of the darkened room, Marla making her way along the corridor. She was alone. Aerial had spent time with that roster and knew Marla was the lone senior on the squad and seniors had their own bank of lockers, in their own section of the building.

Marla reached her locker. She saw the letter attached.

The note she had found in her locker this morning had been short and sweet. Written by a classmate (according to the writer), this classmate said they knew who was causing trouble for her parents and if she stopped by her locker tonight before the game all would be revealed. *COME ALONE! If you involve your parents or the police I won't show up. It will simply be another clue that dies. Don't you want to be the hero that ends this? COME ALONE!*

Marla tore open the envelope.

Go to your game. Maybe you'll even get to play. When the game is over go to your vehicle. If you have done as I asked there will be another envelope under your wiper. Read it and follow instructions.

Marla was distraught. Her hands were shaking so badly she was glad she wouldn't be seeing action unless the team was winning big time.

She sat on the bench watching the volley ball ping pong back and forth accompanied by a lot of grunting and screeching of sneakers. With each point registered, Marla prayed for the match to end. Instead, a seesaw battle ensued with each game ending in an overtime point.

At least it was one of those close matches that guaranteed Marla wouldn't be getting into the fray. She was glad none of her family had come to watch. She had told them she wouldn't see any action and it would be a waste of their time.

Her coach did notice her nervous demeanor and tried to reassure her, Marla said she was fine. "Hoping for a win that's all," she smiled.

The match finally ended. Marla couldn't get out of there quickly enough.

She spotted her car in the lot and in the light from an overhead lamppost immediately saw a white envelope under the wiper.

She grabbed the envelope. She held it to her chest as she opened her car door breathing heavily. She looked left and right for someone lurking. Before entering she carefully checked that no one was hiding in the back seat.

Shaking like a leaf Marla sat behind the wheel locked the doors and turned on the interior light. Her breath began to fog the windshield so she started the car. As the air from the heater blower ruffled her hair she tore open the envelope. The message was brief.

Sit here in the parking lot until it empties, when I'm sure you are alone and you didn't screw me over, I will make myself known.

Marla re-checked that she had locked the doors. She opened her phone ready to dial 911 if necessary. She reached beneath her seat and grabbed a can of mace and her trusty tire thumper given to her by her dad when he gave her the keys to her first car.

Marla had followed orders and told no one of the note in her locker.

She tapped the tire thumper with her fingers as she gazed around the dimly lit parking lot. She raised her eyes to her rearview mirror finding nothing back there but her own eyes.

In that moment she realized the eyes looking back at her were so like her fathers. She nodded to herself, *I can do this.*

Marla sat there for an hour drumming her fingers, switching the radio on and off and feeling her mind race to one ending then another.

Finally the last taillight winked out. She sat there another hour. That hour spent in a daze. The lot was empty now. With each passing minute her thoughts morphed into even more terrifying possibilities.

She continued to scan the parking lot. No movement, no one emerged from the semi-darkness. Marla hadn't moved her body but her eyes had been on full alert. She checked her watch. It was obvious the messenger wasn't going to appear. She turned on her headlights, sighing deeply. *What could all this mean?*

*   *   *

As Aerial sat and watched the girls compete he was struck by the teamwork necessary to keep that stupid ball from hitting the floor.

He had never been a teammate, his only skill had come from standing atop a long piece of wood trying to keep his balance.

In the moment a sense of loneliness and aloneness washed over him like a large wave. He nearly blacked out. He tried to fight the current. Both teams had battled to the end. Then shook hands and complimented one another. Aerial saw a different side of what it means to compete.

As Aerial watched the girl leave the building and head for her car, sudden indecision of what he intended reached his mind. Hidden in the darkness as he waited for the lot to empty he began seeing shadows in his head.

His mother appeared, scolding him for frightening children. His sister showed up laughing at his stupidity even as she stuffed herself, his old man jumped aboard shaking his fist telling him to get a damn job.

Aerial actually spoke aloud to the dark. "I have a job you bastard."

He began to doubt himself. There might be a different way. That different way had revealed itself this morning when checking for more leaks in the trailer. Was it possible? Maybe he didn't need to frighten this girl tonight. He owed it to everyone involved to at least check it out. He knew the man's name from back in the day. As a child he had spent time on his porch.

One final thought cemented his decision. *The man being asked to come up with the money had never been anything other than kind to him and Aerial now might know part of the reason. At least he was pretty sure he did.*

He took a mental detour on his ride home. *The cement had been poured but had yet to harden. A short visit could fix that.*

His bike turned left toward the beach. Trying to think things through as the wheels in his mind churned with the turn of his pedals. He made his way toward Flagler beach.

When he arrived at the bridge spanning the Intercoastal water way, he got off his bike and walked to the apex of the span. The nearly quarter mile walk to the top of the bridge had him winded once again. As his lungs worked overtime so did his brain. He suddenly realized he had put something in motion that he hadn't thought through. Maybe he could fix it after-all.

When he reached the top of the span and looked down at the water below, dark and forbidding he still found no answers. He looked east to the ocean and west to man's version of civilization. In a flash of recollection his mornings on a surf board emerged.

Those were the only happy times of his life. The waves winked in the moonlight as if sending a signal.

He coasted down the decline and reached A1A. He crossed over the road and walked his bike down onto the soft beach sand.

It was dark down here close to the water. No one was about. He sat down. The cool sand was comforting. Clouds skidded across the sky allowing an observer to make of them what they will. The waves lapped the shoreline whispering. Aerial saw his life past, present and future in those sounds and formations.

Nothing in his life had ever stuck. Everything had passed by in half light. In the wave action he heard and felt a stepfather who punished without pause.

In a passing cloud he saw a sister eating herself to death at the kitchen table. His mother appeared in another trying to keep form and hold her family together as she raced through the sky.

Suddenly the sky darkened and ended in a brief passage of rain. Finally as the rain shower passed and the moon reappeared he saw himself in a thin wispy cloud that seemed to have no beginning or end, no structure, you could see right through it.

He began to cry softly into his sleeve. He got up and walked his bike into the water. He walked along with waves lapping him nearly to his waist. The water was cold which numbed him but shocked him to his senses. By the time he left the ocean he had decided and set his new course.

Aerial had grown up in and around water and knew exactly what he was doing for the first time in a long time. He knew what he had to do to finish this.

CHAPTER TWENTY

Steve checked his watch. It was 11:12pm the bar had been busy tonight. Most nights he found time to talk with the patrons which he enjoyed. But tonight it had been just order and delivery.

Then just as things were quieting, right on cue Aerial Steward like an apparition had appeared. He stood behind his favorite stool. His hair was wet and his clothing soggy. When Steve approached him with a beer Aerial waved it away. He didn't sit down he seemed to be on a mission.

If you believe in Karma, well this became a Karma moment.

A Rascal Flatts tune began playing on the jukebox. Steve tuned out the din of noise hanging over the bar like a layer of smoke and listened to the lyrics of one of his favorite songs.

He heard it nearly every night. His regulars pumped in the quarters that three or four times a night prompted raised glasses and promises to themselves that they would act on those words. Aerial turned to listen. He seemed to pay special attention to the words tonight. He had yet to offer a greeting he just stood weaving slowly from side to side in cadence with the words.

I've dealt with my ghosts and I've faced all my demons finally content with a past I regret. I've found you can find strength in your moment of weakness, for once I'm at peace with myself.

I've been burdened with blame trapped in a past for too long. I'm movin on.

Aerial swayed to the music letting the words wash over him. As the next verse began he looked around as if on stage and singing those words himself. I've lived in this place and I know all the faces. Each one is different but they're always the same. They mean me no harm but it's time that I face it they'll never allow me to change. But I never dreamed home would end up where I don't belong, I'm movin on.

In the middle of that song, still soggy wet, Aerial Steward climbed on to the bar stool as if he'd been given one final signal. He did a full spin taking in the world as he'd known it, saluted Steve, rose and as if in a trance, left and closed the door behind him.

Rascal Flatts wasn't finished, perhaps Aerial should have waited.

Forgiveness was part of the lyrics, possibly even a form of redemption. But Aerial Steward had heard enough apparently.

He climbed back on his bike. He raised his eyes to the dark once more and pedaled away.

Where did he intend to go?

What did he intend to do?

Where had he been?

Could Aerial Steward be imagining what the words from the final stanza of that song would look like? Words that spoke of packing up and leaving. Whatever was in his mind, whether choosing door number one or door number two, the thought kept him from looking left or right? His eyes remained on the sky.

On a dark night in Flagler beach, stars gleaming, clouds not done drawing images on the universe's chalkboard, Aerial Steward on his borrowed bicycle crossed the road; directly into the path of an oncoming automobile.

Aerial Steward's bike didn't climb a lawn and end up looking up at a living room ceiling, injured, but repairable, like Wayne Garrett.

The bike was struck broadside sending Aerial into the air. Just as his given name implied he rode the air wave briefly then stuck a head first landing. He was dead in the second.

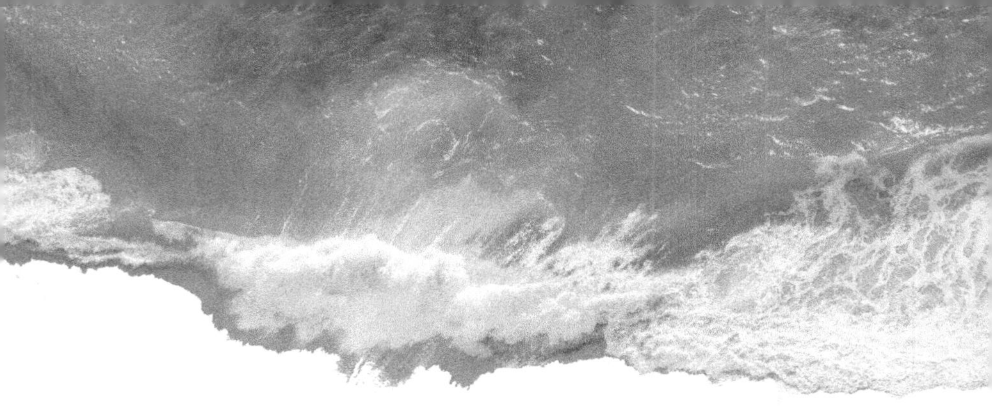

CHAPTER TWENTY-ONE

It was late.

Marla's parents were beside themselves. Marla should have been home hours ago. They had heard sirens blaring an hour ago which fed their concern.

A mere half mile down the road their daughter was sitting in the back of a police SUV with a rag to her nose.

Scrunched up like dirty laundry she managed a look out the passenger window as red and blue flashes of light lit up the darkened street.

Marla never saw the bicycle or its rider. Suddenly her windshield had exploded and her airbag released. The impact dazed her and her nose was bleeding. How she managed to be in the back of a police car she didn't remember. Who handed her the cloth she held over her nose was a mystery. As the colored lights continued to cast shadows, her mind returned to the parking lot at the school.

She recalled sitting for what had seemed hours for her family's nightmare to end. When no one came she recalled starting her car and left the lot. She must have arrived in Flagler Beach but she didn't remember crossing the long Intercoastal Bridge. She suddenly remembered the notes she was bringing to her father. She checked her pocket. As she was about to remove them a man in uniform opened the door to the police vehicle introducing himself.

* * *

A short time later blue lights lit up the living room shade at the Garrett residence.

* * *

Within the hour one of the paramedics first on the scene had finished his shift but wasn't ready to go home. He was trying to forget what he had responded to and seen. His shift had officially ended earlier but here it was nearly 12:00 last call for alcohol at the <u>FISH OR CUT BAIT.</u>

Steve recognized Tyler from his usual 11 pm stop in for a beer before he went home routine. With Tyler it was always a single beer. His job saw too many bad endings that often began with a second beer.

"You're late tonight Tyler. All those sirens I heard earlier the reason?

Tyler nodded somberly. "It was a bad one Steve, I don't think the guy ever knew what hit him. I feel worse for who hit him."

"Any one you knew?"

"The guy was pretty messed up in the face. No wallet on him." He shook his head. "The girl that hit him I recognized from seeing her and her family around town and at the beach. She's the postman's daughter, Wayne Garrett, do you know him?"

Steve couldn't place the name as someone he knew. He was sure he had heard or read the name somewhere though.

Tyler rubbed his forehead, "Odd thing, it didn't really rain tonight, maybe a sprinkle, but when we got there and looked beyond the damage done by that sewer grate, we found that the victim's clothes were soggy wet like the guy had come from a dip in the surf.

Steve's eyes opened wide. He shook his head from side to side like a wet dog, as his mind began making connections. *Holy shit*, he thought.

"Tyler there was a guy in here earlier three stools down from where you are right now, he was soaking wet. That guy was Aerial Steward!"

Steve served Tyler and tried to go about his business but he couldn't keep the image of the very strange actions of a man he saw most every night from entering his mind. He found himself shivering.

Last call ended and Steve closed up. Tyler had told him where the accident happened and Steve drove to the area and parked. Yellow tape was in place, lights were still flashing, and officers were measuring and taking pictures.

Someone, possibly a teenager, looked out from the rear seat window of a police car. The damaged car that had struck Aerial was parked to the side and the mangled bike remained on scene. Steve nodded to himself as the title and the last line of each stanza from the Rascal Flatts hit rewind in his head. <u>I'm movin on.</u>

* * *

When the blue lights hit Wayne's driveway Wayne and Becky looked at one another thinking the worst.

They looked out the window as an officer stepped from his vehicle. The man studied their house. A lump entered Wayne's throat as he prepared himself for the worst. The officer turned and opened the back door of a police vehicle and their oldest daughter emerged holding a white cloth to the side of her face.

Hunched, and in that moment at least, shrunken and visibly aged their daughter Marla took a deep breath and followed the officer. Becky and Wayne too took deep breaths and raced to the door.

Becky made it to her daughter still navigating the driveway and folded her into her arms. The girl could not speak she simply hung onto her mother as Wayne reached her and added his own two arms.

They made it to the porch and the girl collapsed into a chair. The officer walked behind with hat still in hand. Wayne nodded.

He had spoken with this man a number of times over the past months. This same officer had been personally helpful recently.

Flagler Beach Police Chief Dennis Cusack respectfully waited as the family found their bearings. He walked to the railing and looked out over the darkened yard.

The dark magic of night time was not lost on him. When he looked up he could see the stars in all their splendor. The moon had emerged and was right where it was supposed to be. Cloud formations were drawing images across God's creation.

When he looked straight ahead into the foliage however, he saw and heard the reality of what darkness and mankind brought to his work.

People generally acted out their worst best selves after dark. The muggings, domestic assaults, the screaming accusations, the thievery, overdoses, and auto accidents all bathed in blood, took place within the blackened hedges. He nodded to himself and sighed.

When things had quieted he found that two younger daughters had joined them. He took a seat for himself and with all eyes on him he began to explain what had apparently happened.

"Your daughter was simply in the wrong place at what became the wrong time for a man who obviously drove directly into the path of her vehicle."

He held his hat in his hands as he continued, "We haven't identified him as yet but since he was on a bicycle we believe he was a local."

* * *

Marla didn't attend school the next morning but word had already reached there. By morning all the kids from Flagler Beach had heard at least fragments of what had happened though they lacked specifics.

Marla Garrett their classmate was somehow connected or so they had heard. By lunchtime more specifics had reached the rumor mill and the lunchroom buzzed with the knowledge that someone had been killed in an accident though no one seemed to know who.

The phone at the Garrett residence was off the hook and Marla herself was not answering her cell.

In the afternoon and evening, Facebook and Twitter lit up. When the students reached school the next morning, there was still no Marla there to clarify anything. Some facts however had reached school officials.

There would be a brief assembly this morning to start the day. When the student body all reached the bleacher seats, the Principal took to the wireless mike in the middle of the gym. A basket of flowers sat on a folding table at his side. Behind him six janitors sat in folding chairs.

"I've asked you all to come together to remember and honor one of our own."

The student body seemed confused and buzzed about it.

The Principal held up his hand and things quieted. "Aerial Steward had only been a Janitor in this building for a short time but somehow I'm sure he impacted at least a few of you."

A buzz arose from the bleachers as kids compared notes.

His hand rose once again, "You might have seen him in the corridors picking up after you, or sweeping up what you dropped during lunch."

Coach Snyder thought she had seen him attending the volleyball game several nights earlier and spoke up.

The principal smiled wanly, "So it seems Aerial Steward had truly taken an interest in all the good things that happen here."

He took a deep breath. "Let's bow our heads. Aerial Steward you are not forgotten you'll always be a Palm Coast Bulldog."

The bleachers emptied and the buzz was all about who in hell was Aerial Steward. In death as in life, Aerial Steward remained invisible.

But at this moment in time he had become immortalized forever after as a <u>Palm Coast High School Bulldog</u>. Aerial Steward had finally become a member of a team.

A short article in the Observer, when it reached the public several days later, noted the accident and included just the briefest of obituaries.

The article would not get attached to a refrigerator but it did catch the eye of a man who had once known him; Wayne Garrett.

Wayne had been given the name by the Sheriff the day after the accident but the reality of it set in when he saw it in print.

Aerial Steward, 54 of Flagler Beach, Florida, was killed when he was hit riding his bicycle late at night. He apparently crossed directly into the path of a car being driven by a Flagler Beach resident. (Marla's name was not mentioned.)

From what the Observer was able to piece together Mr. Steward had only recently returned to his home town and even more recently taken a job as a Janitor at Palm Coast High School. He left no living relatives that this paper could find for comment.

* * *

Marla tried to make the trip back to normalcy. For the first few days she and her sisters stayed home from school and as a family they found strength in one another. When a week later Wayne received a call from Mr. Jamie Collins he made his way to the retirement home.

"Come in Wayne." Jamie began their lengthy conversation with a bit of Irish insight. "Nobody knows where his sod of death is."

Wayne found a comfortable chair. It was clear his old mentor had more wisdom to impart.

"Here's a riddle for you to wrestle with Wayne. When is it that the end can be the beginning and the beginning the end?"

Wayne had no idea what was coming next so like a shoe suspended from striking the floor he simply waited.

"He called me that night." When Wayne remained stymied Jamie added. "Aerial." Jamie paused. "He did. The very night he died."

Wayne's heart quickened. What was Jamie telling him?

Another Irish quip found its way into the room. "The wearer best knows where the shoe pinches." He let that settle then Jamie continued.

"The man confessed all his sins. Some of those sins concerned you and your family." Jamie nodded. "So I believe it is safe to say your turmoil is over, well at least the part that threatens your family. Mine continues."

Wayne had a million thoughts filling his head but simply asked, "Did he say why my family was his target?"

Once more Jamie Collins led with an Irish proverb. "The pen's trace remains though the hand that held it dies."

When Wayne offered a blank look Jamie explained. "Aerial's life was not an easy one and he chose the path that offered the least effort and resistance. He didn't have to look too far afield to see that you chose a different path."

Wayne remained confused and his furrowed brow led to Jamie's next line.

"Remember your first paper route."

Wayne nodded.

"Aerial told me he carried an anger from an early age that he never let go of. When he returned here and read of your heroics saving a child from drowning his pent up anger of being passed over for something as simple as a paper route all those years ago burst like a potato in a microwave."

"Why did he call you with all this?"

Jamie shook his head solemnly, "Before that call that might have been a million dollar question."

The two men sat in silence. Jamie Collins continued to wrestle his hands.

Wayne could see Jamie was still troubled and not finished, "Can I make you a cup of coffee Jamie, I don't think you're done with your story are you?"

Jamie simply shook his head, "Just getting started really."

"One question first though, did Aerial intend to end his life that night? If so why did he choose you to tell?"

Over the next hour Wayne was told a story. A story that revealed an Irish tragedy. Wayne left with a simple request from the man who had given Wayne and his family so much. A request that would open up a whole new world for the Garrett family.

PART TWO

CHAPTER TWENTY-TWO

Forgiveness would be the first hurdle. Marla was the most difficult to convince that she should offer forgiveness to a man who had nearly destroyed their lives. Though the man was dead nightmares continued to invade her sleep.

When her father returned from visiting Jamie Collins he confirmed the man had not intended to ride into her path.

"According to Jamie Aerial fully intended to leave town after that night of reflection and confession."

"Mr. Collins told you that?" asked Marla.

"In his own way he did. Of course he had to use his own translation of an Irish proverb. '**Better tonight than tomorrow morning,**' he said.

Aerial told him of watching you Marla, playing volley ball, at lunch, in the corridors, and in that parking lot. In the dark, a moment surfaced in his mind that suggested your innocence in all this. He became disgusted with himself for scaring you girls.

"It was also in that conversation with Mr. Collins that Aerial mentioned what he intended to do the very next morning."

Becky spoke up. "What's the connection? Why did he call Jamie?"

Wayne offered the big reveal, "Because Aerial Steward had a son."

"Okay, and what does that have to do with Jamie Collins?"

Wayne took a deep breath. "Because Jamie Collins had a son as well."

Wayne took an even deeper breath, "his name was Aerial Steward!" He let that sit a moment. "Though the boy was not known to Jamie at birth nor for a long time after."

Becky was confused and shocked, "I thought Jamie never married."

"He didn't but apparently he met someone once. One night in the city of racing fame. He didn't see the woman again until a few years later when he found her living in the tenement house he inherited. He met her son but had no idea Aerial was his own."

The women all shook their heads in disbelief.

Wayne waited out the half questions being asked.

Becky finally asked, "Did Aerial tell Jamie where the boy, Jamie's grandson lives?"

That opened the flood gates with one question following another. "Is the boy with his mother? Does the boy know he has a grandfather?"

The questions continued to fly back and forth like that recent volley-ball game. Wayne had few return volleys.

Though he did manage, "I doubt the boy knows of Jamie. Aerial himself was going to need to re-introduce himself to his son."

Becky was about to ask how Aerial lost track of his son when Wayne put up his hands. "Jamie didn't go into any detail, he was focused on finding his grandson."

"So where are we in all this?" Becky asked.

"Well Jamie knows the boy's given name. It mirrors the strange surfing names_Aerial _and his sister Bailing, were given. His grandson is named Ripper."

Dorothy the youngest daughter scrunched her brow. "What does that even mean?"

"Aerial told Jamie the name describes a very good surfer. Aerial revealed the name with pride in his voice, Jamie told me."

"So Aerial didn't know until recently that Jamie Collins was his father?"

"Apparently not. When Aerial called he told Jamie from a letter he found in the wall of his trailer his mother indicated Jamie Collins was his father. He wanted nothing from him. He just needed to clear his mind of things before he moved on.

He thanked Jamie for all he had tried to do for him when he was a boy. 'I should have listened to you Mr. Collins. My mother, in that letter she never sent to you, told the whole story."

Jamie said he tried to speak but Aerial shushed him and told him it wasn't his fault. "I'm not angry but I could use your help." It was then he told Jamie of a son he intended to reconnect with. "I need to do better than was done to me.'" Jamie promised to help in any way he could.

So Jamie from a distance watched Aerial choose a path he himself couldn't support. Not knowing it was his son he was offering possibilities to. He said had he known he would have tried harder. In the end Aerial tried on the margins but had stronger influences directing him.

"That night according to Jamie it seemed both men were attempting to turn all that around. As Jamie said, <u>Better tonight than tomorrow morning</u>."

"Aerial told Jamie he needed to sleep on all this and would call again in the morning, visit if that was okay to map out a plan for moving forward."

Wayne was about finished. "Jamie told me he would do whatever it took to find his grandson."

Wayne sighed deeply, "Well tomorrow morning never arrived for Aerial and now we are left to help Jamie with his quest."

"He never did tell Jamie where his son was living?" asked Becky.

"I don't think he knew himself, but he fully intended to bring the boy back to Flagler Beach to introduce him to his grandfather."

CHAPTER TWENTY-THREE

The holidays came and went, hardly celebrated in the Garrett household.

Wayne was back at work and the girls returned to school. Marla was refusing to drive so the girls were taking the bus.

The buzz on social media died down around the incident but Marla couldn't get that night out of her mind as odd looks continued to follow her to the lunch table.

The corridor seemed to quiet whenever she appeared. Marla had shut down her on-line social life but she still had to attend school.

She knew much more about the man who had tried to ruin their family than she could share and had to bite her tongue. So she shut her mouth and remained angry.

To Marla it seemed Aerial Steward and the manner of his death was one more attack on her family. This was her senior year of high school and she should be enjoying the lessening of pressure and be thinking about college. Instead she was experiencing recurring nightmares.

Even as she did her studies in the quiet of the evening and tried to fit in at lunch pasting on a smile, she couldn't shake the shadow of the man. Whenever a Janitor neared her lunch table she would flinch, they all wore the face of Aerial Steward.

Nights were the worst though, Aerial Steward continued to invade her sleep. In her mind's eye she saw the man actually smile as he passed directly above her field of vision before crashing to the pavement. Suddenly wide awake, not knowing she had cried out, her two sisters arrived at her bed and hugged her, she was a ball of sweat.

Her sisters tried to get her to talk to them but Marla did not want them to experience anymore of the man who had kidnapped them and scared them nearly to death.

In reality each of the sisters was experiencing their own horrors.

* * *

When spring arrived and Jamie Collins had made no headway in finding Aerial's son, Wayne mentioned the difficulty Jamie was experiencing.

Becky thought the family had heard just about enough on the whole topic. Wayne said he felt an obligation but didn't know how he could help.

For some reason the idea of doing something struck a chord with Marla. She felt she was going through the motions, numb to everything; unfinished business.

She wrote to herself in her diary and arrived at a decision. She called the Flagler Beach Police Department.

She was ushered into Chief Dennis Cusack's office and sat facing a desk that was covered with family pictures. Chief Cusack had been kind and understanding throughout the whole mess. He had even introduced the family to a form of healing. Those outings in a kayak had helped Marla immensely.

* * *

The lawn of the Garrett house was set up for a celebration. On the driveway was a poster and balloons announcing that this home contained a High School Graduating Senior.

Proud mom Becky, moved among the tables with a pitcher of lemonade and a big smile on her face. Her first born had reached a milestone. She looked around spotting her husband Wayne sitting at a table with a man who had become a good friend, Police Chief Dennis Cusack.

Smiles had replaced the air of concern that originally brought the two men together.

In the days following the death of Aerial Steward and the ending of the drama the Sheriff introduced Wayne and oldest daughter Marla to kayaking. After that first trip both Wayne and Marla confessed they had never seen Florida in its true innocence. It took some time for Marla to not see a reflection of Aerial Steward in every paddle stroke. For a time she imagined sweeping his face below the water only to see it bob back up as she switched to the opposite side of the kayak. The peacefulness of the venue could not be ignored however and she began spending more time watching the wildlife and foliage reveal itself. Finally Aerial stayed below the surface. Not forgotten but not right in her face.

Kayaking became a healing for the inner part of Wayne's body and Marla's mind.

Those kayak trips and visits to Jamie Collins led to the first pronouncement of forgiveness for the man who had caused all the trouble. They had also led Marla to the sheriff's office.

That evening after all the guests were gone and the family sat around a small fire in the back yard Marla looked deep into the flames and made her announcement. "I'm going to take a year off before I go to college."

Her parents sat up straighter in their bag chairs.

"Hear me out before you freak out," she began calmly.

* * *

Six months to the day of hitting and fatally injuring Aerial Steward, Marla spent the morning packing. Family friend and benefactor Jamie Collins had given Marla a slightly used SUV for a graduation present, replacing the badly damaged little Ford Fiesta that was eight years used when Marla had received it.

After sitting with Wayne and hearing of how the entire episode involving Aerial was affecting Marla, Jamie Collins asked Wayne to send Marla to speak with him.

The retirement home had a porch and it was there in one of the rockers that Jamie Collins felt most comfortable. He was sitting there rocking, pretending to read a newspaper when Marla walked up. "I can see anger and confusion in your body language lassie, come and sit with an old man."

Marla sighed deeply and sat down not knowing what the closest to a grandfather she'd ever known, would have to say.

"Let your anger of all that's happened set with the sun and not rise again. I allowed anger at my own father to ride my shirt-tail for the longest time. It did me no favor."

"Jamie, I can't help it, that man tried to ruin our family."

Jamie took her hand and turned it palm up. "See all the little creases in your palm, girl. Each one is a possible path for you to follow." He began tracing a line that began near the palm and offered the straightest path to her fingers. "That line is a river. God intended that line to be a guide for your hands to follow." He looked deep into Marla's eyes and continued.

"Some of those little lines are like streams that might have you wandering but will eventually bring you back to the river."

He looked into her eyes and smiled. "Still others are like eddies swirling and muddying the waters of your life and offer nothing more than confusion and heartbreak." Jamie sat back and released Marla's hand.

"You learned recently that Aerial Steward was my son." Jamie looked straight at Marla, "that lads' palm contained no straight lines, just a series of eddies."

Marla need more.

"I know you're wrestling with all that's come about. Perhaps you could benefit from putting that fine mind to proper use." An Irish proverb followed. "An old broom knows the dirty corners best."

Marla had no idea what Jamie was getting at.

Jamie made it all come clear. "I'm too old and feeble to play detective but if you could find it within yourself to track down my grandson I'll offer any support and wisdom I still have to help in your search."

He handed her a package and followed with a suggestion. "Go see your police chief I've known him for years. He's a good family man and I hear he's already been a benefit to your family."

"Where would I even start?"

"I think the ocean would be a good starting point and talk with the chief, its well-known Aerial was involved with the law a good deal of his life."

* * *

Marla told Chief Cusack that throughout his life, Aerial loved being around water. She mentioned the menial jobs Aerial had filled and the lifestyle Aerial had lived.

The chief had been very helpful when Marla approached him with her plan. He agreed that this quest could be part of her healing and he would make inquiries with fellow law enforcement that might offer a road map of the county jails Aerial had turned up in over the years.

* * *

Sisters Shellee and Dorothy offered tearful goodbyes and lingering hugs. Mom and Dad put on a brave face but had already begun to add worry lines.

Marla closed the door and dragged her single suitcase to her SUV. Armed with a roadmap of the east coast portion of the country, red circles surrounded a series of beach towns. Fortified with a travel mug of a recently acquired taste for coffee, Marla was ready to begin her road trip.

The SUV Jamie had gifted her for graduation gleamed in the morning light. Marla checked the map. Her Flagler Beach home located in the north central part of Florida left her with a choice. North or South.

Aerial had left a trail from New Smyrna Beach, a short trip to the south in Volusia County, to Jacksonville in the northern part of Florida, then further north to North Carolina, possibly all the way to Virginia.

Marla looked to her passenger seat that held her handbag and the life line given her by Jamie Collins. Within her purse was an ample amount of money and a credit card.

Chief Cusack supplied a contact to every County Sheriff that bordered the Atlantic Ocean from Florida to Virginia.

With promises of calls every night from her sisters, and the knowledge that her parents would be staying in touch, Marla left her little town of Flagler Beach and turned west onto route 100.

She crossed the Intercoastal waterway, a daily route she had traveled for years on a bus. This morning she didn't pass under Interstate 95 but rather turned left onto the highway that stretches from Maine to Miami.

Forty minutes later she exited Interstate 95 and turned left once again east toward New Smyrna Beach. She drummed her fingers on the steering wheel as one easy listening tune after another filled the quiet apprehension she was feeling. Unlike the tunes offered up in the dark parking lot that night, today the tunes seemed lively hopeful even.

She turned off the radio and pulled to the side of the road. She turned on the navigation app on her phone. She was to follow directions to 101 Canal Street. Flagler Beach Police Chief Dennis Cusack had made contact with the sheriff of Volusia County.

A day later a return call indicated Aerial Steward had once been arrested in new Smyrna Beach, spending two days in their facility then processed into the Daytona Beach Jail, the main jail for Volusia County.

Marla was given the name of the lieutenant who headed this satellite facility.

She took a deep breath and opened the door of her vehicle. She looked back once to push the key fob as if to lock out the past then pushed against the glass door that would start her future.

A heavy set lady was fiddling with her own I Phone when Marla announced herself. The lady put down her phone long enough to make contact with someone and Marla was directed to take a seat.

She studied the walls and the floor and the ceiling. Just as she was beginning a second pass of the architecture she was summoned and ushered into the office of Lieutenant Brian White.

The man stood as Marla entered. She watched as the big man unfolded. She could practically hear his bones creaking. A shaved head gleamed as it edged closer and closer to the light fixture. Marla recognized an athlete when she saw one. This large black man crossed the room and engulfed her hand in an instant. A smile amplified by very white teeth and that huge hand invited her to sit.

"Your Chief told me you'd be stopping in. How can I help?" He found his way back behind his desk then faced her with a big smile.

Marla, who had been worrying how she would be received was put immediately at ease.

She began. "I'm on kind of a magical mystery tour and don't even have a ticket to ride." She sighed aloud. "So I'll just tell you what I know and hopefully you can fill in some spaces."

The Lieutenant smiled and nodded. "Do tell."

Marla referred to a small notebook that had suddenly appeared in her hand. She offered the date that Aerial Steward had been arrested by the Beach Patrol and the date he left New Smyrna Beach to transfer to the jail in Daytona.

Lieutenant Brian white nodded. "After the call from your Chief Cusack I took the liberty of reviewing his ask." Lieutenant White opened a folder. He began reading aloud.

"Aerial Steward was ticketed on a number of occasions both on the beach for being intoxicated in public and brawling at some of the local bars. Written warnings were handed out on four different occasions."

The Lieutenant looked up, "Have you heard the old adage, **if you're always crawling through a dumpster you're going to leave with a smell?**"

Marla simply nodded, she got it.

The Lieutenant looked back at his folder. "From Aerial Stewards interaction with this department I would venture that he was here and there in New Smyrna for about a year and six months. When we caught him breaking into a local business he was sent from here to the Volusia County jail and we never saw again.

"When he was first arrested did anyone show up to try to try to get him released?"

Lieutenant White rubbed his chin, "What are you looking for specifically?"

Marla sighed, "I'm not really sure. All I know is before Aerial died he told someone he had a son. The someone he told, is the boy's grandfather. I'm trying to find the boy."

Lieutenant White, shifted his weight forward but said nothing.

"Aerial Steward spent his life moving from one surfing town to another. His criminal record is kind of the roadmap I'm using to solve this. New Smyrna Beach is my first stop."

The lieutenant looked back into the folder. "There was a woman who showed up. She was drunk and ended up being charged herself but we later let her go. I do have a name. This was years ago though, not sure she's even still around."

Marla left with a final handshake, a name, Cindy Strout, and a possible address.

Sitting back in her vehicle she wondered, *is this going be this easy?* She plugged in the address and let her onboard navigator guide her to 358 South Broad Street apt. 9.

The apartment complex was three stories high and in disrepair. Several children were playing on the sidewalk. Two little girls were drawing in chalk while a third, a boy, seemed to be harassing the two.

Marla parked at the curb and walked across a small patch of weedy lawn. *Dad wouldn't let our lawn look like this,* she thought. The children didn't look up as she passed but the little girls referred to the boy as Brian as they shouted at him to leave them alone.

Marla found the right apartment number on the second floor. She knocked. She looked back toward the street from a very narrow porch that didn't even have room to place a chair. A fringe of weeds marked the beginning of the sidewalk. Marla who grew up with both a front and back lawn to play on, thought to herself, *I couldn't live here.* She knocked once more.

The door was opened by a woman who appeared to be early middle age, her hair all askew. She was wearing a faded black-tee shirt with features from a band Marla had never heard of. Her belly stretched the fabric and her nakedness below was open to the breeze, Marla had to look away.

Marla waited a beat then looked back and down at slippers sporting bunny ears with black glassy eyes. When Marla raised her own eyes the eyes looking back at her were as vacant as the bunny's.

The woman appeared anxious, rubbing her hands together while searching for words that wouldn't come. The lady finally managed a muffled, "I heard you knocking."

Marla said, "I'm looking for Cindy Strout"

A furrowed brow looked down on a mouth that was just now opening. Dentures clacked with her words. "She was my sister. She used to live here." The words came out like watching ice melt; one drip at a time.

"Do you know where she is?"

"Dead!" The woman's eyes widened.

At that moment the boy from below, Brian, appeared at the door. His eyes were bright with anticipation. "Cincy and Rachel are going to get ice cream, can I have a dollar?"

"You little shit." Her eyes narrowed, "you think just cause we have company I'm going to play nice?" She cocked her head like a rooster studying a worm before swallowing it whole. "Maybe you should treat me a little better when there's no one around."

She fluttered her hands, "Go scrounge your own money." All the ice had melted and the words appeared as an open faucet. Clacking noises amplified her anger. Her glassy eyes had cleared long enough to focus her venom.

The boy skulked off with head hanging. Words left his mouth just below a level that might lead to a slap upside the head.

The woman hmmphed and redirected her attention to Marla with no attempt to hide her naked lower body.

Marla didn't have the opportunity to redirect the conversation before the woman finished with a flourish. 'My sister is dead. Overdose. That was her little shit you just met. The father is dead too. They died in each-other's arms." She smiled but not with warmth. "Isn't that romantic. Now I have to raise the kid."

Marla felt for the woman but realized she was out of her depth. She asked just one more question before apologizing for disturbing the woman and hurried away.

A flood of emotions followed her back to the street where the two girls were just now gathering their chalk. The boy was standing alone sulking. Marla spoke to him on her way by. The boy responded by asking Marla for a dollar.

Marla stopped in her tracks and really took in what she was experiencing. She noticed the shabbiness of the clothing the kids were wearing, their dirty bare feet. She looked once more at the condition of the apartment building, one of five that lined the street. She sighed and opened her purse. She handed each of the three a five dollar bill. Their eyes lit up and they left running to wherever not bothering with a thank you ma'am. The one thought that reached Marla felt uncharitable. *I wonder how long those five dollar bills will be in their hands.*

Marla needed to regroup and re-think all this. She had so many unanswered possibilities running through her head she needed to take a moment. The last question asked assured Marla that the sister who died did not mother Aerial's child. She got back in her SUV and sat there for a time.

Suddenly she needed nourishment on many levels. Marla drove to the tourist section of town where she spotted a café sign. She parked and walked into a very different café environment than she was used to.

Several overstuffed chairs with little tables at their side like a parlor scene seemed to beckon her. She walked up to the counter and read the menu. Sandwiches and pastries galore dominated a blackboard. Six different coffee choices and several hot or cold drink concoctions were listed.

Marla ordered a Tuna on Rye with Swiss cheese and sprouts. She studied the coffee choices. Her own introduction to caffeine began at the kitchen table back when the family was being threatened.

Lots of long conversations after her two younger sisters had gone to bed introduced her to the amber liquid that seemed to draw her closer still to her parents.

Cream and sugar was on a table and as she stirred both into her drink she looked into the muddy waters and sighed deep in her chest.

The over-stuffed chairs were vacant and she sat down to reflect on this mission she was undertaking.

Aerial had lived a nomadic under the radar alcohol fueled existence. If this morning was any indication she would be seeing much more of the underbelly of these beach towns. Did she have the courage to finish this, she asked herself?

In her head she took stock of who she was. *I'm 18, live in a nice neighborhood, have a supportive family, have never been involved in anything that included the police until my family was threatened, Dad has always been our fearless leader, is this a test I want to take?*

Just by asking those very questions Marla was moving beyond girlhood and becoming a strong young woman. The more she thought about it her Dad was more than a leader, he had been subtly training his daughters since the day they were born.

Her first memory of her dad was when he challenged her to take that first step into outstretched arms, later her dad running behind her as she learned to ride a bike. She recalled the day a leap of faith sent her off the side of a dock, followed by a dozen other firsts that became routine. She took out her phone and dialed him up.

As she was listening to her father offering encouragement, a young man entered the café and with coffee in hand took the overstuffed chair facing her. She glanced but didn't really take notice. She actually turned away slightly to finish her conversation with her dad.

When she ended the call she turned back around and looked directly at a paper coffee cup raised to the drinking position covering the facial features of the man.

Slowly the cup was lowered and two piercing green eyes met hers. Her breath caught. To herself she thought, *you might just be the handsomest man I have never met.*

As if reading her thoughts those eyes changed from piercing to smiling to downright dancing with merriment. Without a moment's hesitation a hand reached out and the whitest teeth possible emerged offering a name. "I am Crofton Crocker, and who would you be, lass?"

Marla heard an accent in that first sentence that she immediately identified with a documentary she had seen about the Irish River dancers. Her family's benefactor Jamie Collins spoke in this same manner.

She offered her own hand and introduced herself. Maybe it was something in the comfort of the two overstuffed chairs, or was it his eyes, or his snow white teeth; at any rate she felt as mesmerized as Little Red Riding Hood ignoring the dangers of the big bad wolf.

An hour passed in which coffee cooled and was replenished. Marla told her life story. She didn't mention the specific mission she was on at first but it eventually found its way from one overstuffed chair to the other.

Crofton was a good listener. When Marla finished, Crofton took his time in responding to all he had heard.

"There is evil possible at every turn of the road yet we don't cower in the dark. It seems your family addressed it head on and you seem the better for it." He took a bite of a pastry swallowed it with a sip of coffee and continued.

"I don't have a mission like you do facing me. I have finished the one thing I was charged with. I have visited my great-great grandparent's graves. Beyond that I don't have a care in the world." He took a sip of his coffee.

"I do have a famous relative. Well famous in some circles at any rate." He paused and took a sip of an ever cooling beverage.

Echoing the Lieutenant at the New Smyrna Beach police department, Marla simply said, "Do tell."

"Back in 1798 my namesake, T. Crofton Crocker was born in Ireland. He arguably was the man who compiled and gave universal life to what we call <u>Folk Tales</u>." He threw up his hands and laughed aloud.

"Anyway here I am straight off the boat. Now landed in New Smyrna Beach, Florida, my mission complete putting my best foot forward in the gaze of a beautiful lady. Luck of the Irish I would say."

That hour spent somehow formed a friendship that found Crofton Crocker in the passenger seat when Marla made the decision to continue her mission and head north.

They stopped at the motel where Crofton was staying and picked up a suitcase and a back pack and were soon on Interstate 95 north. "I have to make one stop for proper introductions to my family then we'll be on our way, if it suits you."

Crofton cradling a coffee to go was already comfortable with the arrangement and simply smiled. He made himself at home and dialed up a station that was offering up word filled ballads rather than the loose lyrics of pop music.

During the ride he lowered the volume and began to fill in the gaps of what his namesake had done to advance and promote the <u>Irish Folktale</u>.

"The original T. Crofton Crocker is a wee bit famous in our part of the world." He turned off the radio and tried to draw a parallel to what Marla was trying to do. "You seem to be trying to connect the dots in this mystery of finding someone who might or might not exist in a place you have never traveled to."

Crofton turned even further in Marla's direction, "Crofton Crocker was doing something similar. He traveled a much smaller world seeking the unknown origins of tales told at night over fire pits, in drinking houses, kitchens, and at the foot of the bed over generations, in many lands. Many of these tales seemed to have no distinct author."

Marla continued to have her hands on the wheel and her eyes on the road.

"Are you at all interested in all this blather?"

When Marla insisted he continue, Crofton did just that.

"The common theme in these tales seemed to be cold nights, strong winds, warmth of a fire, darkness, howls in the night, hauntings, and bleakness of landscape. All fodder for stories that provide a bit of entertainment to both family and traveler."

When Marla interrupted Crofton to announce the exit they were about to take, Crofton shut up.

They left Interstate 95 and turned right toward Flagler beach.

CHAPTER TWENTY-FOUR

Four states north in the town of Virginia Beach, Virginia on a street coveted by the surfing community, a young man stood on the corner watching all the girls go by. His name was Jack. At least that's what his friends called him; "Jack the Ripper."

At nineteen years of age he was blessed with several qualities that for the moment seemed to be in high demand.

He could ride a wave like a cowboy coming out of a chute, and he had a smile that wouldn't quit.

He lived a nomadic life and had long ago left any semblance of family behind. Jack lived in a single room over the tavern he worked in nightly.

When asked about any future plans whether by a bar patron, a fellow surfer, or one of the many young women begging to hang on his arm, Jack would utter a line he'd heard somewhere; "I'm just gonna follow the tide, man, find that one big wave."

It seemed enough for Jack, to roll out of a bed that was stripped to the mattress, a sleeping bag he could enter at night, and leave in a lump till his return.

Jack, whose real name in fact was, "Ripper" had no idea he was at the early stage of following a family tradition. One that left unchecked, had led two generations of family down a path to self-destruction.

With the morning sun beginning to shine through a layer of fog and the ocean regaining a glisten to its blue eye that matched the color of his own, he nursed his first cup of coffee and any feeling of same-old, same-old dissipated.

A long mane of sun bleached hair rode his bronzed shoulders, shoulders that stretched well beyond the faded sleeveless tee shirt. If one didn't know the origin of his name they might think it described the entire physique of the young man; he was 'ripped' indeed.

Hailed by fellow surfers as they made their way to the beach carrying their boards, his smile and head nod of affirmation seemed to bolster their own spirits.

"Jack the Ripper" re-opened the letter that had arrived in yesterday's mail.

His father had been killed in a small town in Florida. Hit by a vehicle in the dead of night. The letter had been sent by Jack's mother who he had not seen in several years.

A card on his birthday and a 100 bucks at Christmas was their only contact. His mother now lived on the outskirts of Jacksonville, Florida married for the fourth time; this time to a retired cop. Jack had never met him.

The obituary from the paper was included. In the letter. For the first time his mother told him he had a living breathing Grandfather if he was interested. **'Your father contacted me shortly before he was killed. He said he was involved in a scheme to raise some money he wanted you to have. I figured this was just more of** the same bull-shit he had run past me for years. But this time he actually sounded serious. Said he was screwing with a family that could provide a future for himself and you if you are interested. He mentioned a man who he was pretty sure would pay to protect the family.. He mentioned his name, Jamie Collins. He wanted you to meet him. He said the man had been nice to him when he was a boy.

Not long after, I received a letter from an old friend telling me of your father's death.

Thought you ought to know.

Your mother

Jack was re-reading the obituary when a voice reached out to him. "C'mon Ripper we have miles to surf before we sleep."

Jack folded the letter and the news article, stuffing them in the back pocket of his cutoffs discarded his cup and ran to join his friend.

* * *

Many miles to the south in the small beach town of Flagler Beach, Marla and her new friend Crofton had spent the night at her parent's house.

Marla's younger sisters both instantly fell in love with the green eyed Irishman. The family sat around a back yard fire pit in the quiet of an evening and Crofton regaled them with Irish Folklore inspired by his ancestors.

Wayne remembered his own mother when he was very young telling him similar stories of fairies and pixie dust and things that go bump in the night and nodded in memory.

Marla listened and watched this young man who seemed so comfortable in his own skin mesmerize her family. He seemed years older than the boys she had gone to school with.

She watched the body language of her mother, the family skeptic, relax and begin to laugh and clap her hands in tandem with her daughters.

This morning, fresh off a breakfast of eggs and bacon and toast, all washed down with cups of coffee, Marla and Crofton were off to meet the wizard. The wizard being one Jamie Collins, the man responsible for this mission.

Marla looked briefly to the man sitting beside her in the passenger seat. Their eyes met. Crofton smiled, his eyes dancing with the excitement of meeting the Garrett family benefactor, an Irishman to boot.

Last evening Wayne had told his own story. The girls heard for the first time how Jamie Collins and his mother had been soul mates separated by circumstance.

Wayne brought out the ring he had been given years ago on a porch that was the scene of so many conversations.

"Crofton you remind me of those days on the porch with the rocking chair moving to the beat of whatever bit of wisdom Jamie was trying to impart at the moment."

* * *

The room was dark. Framed in the rectangle of light from the corridor, their eyes searched and a voice reached them. "Is it the angels I'm joining or do I have visitors?" When Marla and Crofton entered the room and snapped on the lamp, Jamie studied them briefly. "Do you have news? Is this my grandson?"

Marla crossed and touched his hand. "No, sorry Jamie but I do have a new friend." She introduced Crofton who bowed and shook Jamie's hand.

"I'm pleased to meet you Crofton, and as well you know, two shorten the road."

Crofton spoke then and the accent that reached Jamie's ears brought tears to his eyes.

"An Irishman! God favors your voyage Marla."

Over the next half hour they exchanged all that Jamie could add that might be helpful then left the man in peace with a smile on his face.

Once more the SUV headed in a northerly direction.

* * *

"Jack the Ripper" spent the morning on his board. Even as he maintained his balance and strutted his stuff his mind was elsewhere.

He hadn't wasted his time thinking about his father in a very long time. And now apparently the man was past tense.

Suddenly it seemed important to find that one big wave that all surfers crave. That one giant wall of water that you enter as a tunnel. A tunnel that would take you to that place some describe as Nirvana.

The wave Jack was thinking of had nothing to do with the water but rather a search for himself. *Could it be that he had a benefactor? He certainly didn't in most respects have a father, or a mother for that matter. Should I seek the man out? Had his father made contact?*

Suddenly Jack lost his balance and ate dirt as he tumbled beneath the wave. He came up sputtering, reminding himself that the ocean doesn't give a rats ass about you or your problems; it just does what it does.

That evening in the bar between serving beers and bullshit to the troubled masses he revisited the letter.

If I was to look, where would that be? He remembered as a kid living in a number of beach towns, in three different states. He was born in Florida that much he knew. And apparently his father died in a small beach town. Maybe that would be a good place to start.

Great surfing in Florida he had been told. That would be a bonus. By the time the bar closed he had done two things. He had quit his job and he had written back to his mother.

Straight forward and direct; I'm coming to Jacksonville. We need to have a long conversation.

Your son.

CHAPTER TWENTY-FIVE

Wayne and Becky resumed their nightly walks. Sometimes daughters' Shellee and Dorothy walked with them but the two girls had been changed forever by the experiences of the past year and often preferred to stay home in their own rooms.

Shellee turned fifteen and was now walking the same hallways in the school her older sister Marla had walked less than a year ago.

Dorothy had entered middle school, always a challenging transition. The two sisters talked nightly and both had begun to keep personal ledgers that were under lock and key.

The recent visit of their older sister, Marla and her new companion Crofton had the two sisters thinking, talking, and writing about boys.

Shellee still harbored a deep seated anger for the disruption that changed the family.

Dorothy was still having nightmares. She sobbed quietly into her pillow upon awakening and shared none of her anguish with anyone.

* * *

Life has a way of coming at you in bunches. Wayne and Becky had new things to share on their walks.

Wayne had undergone numerous tests as his body healed. In a recent blood test, signs of something possibly worrisome had showed up. A follow-up MRI revealed a possible tumor in Wayne's chest. Tomorrow Wayne would go to see the doctor who diagnoses and treats such things.

So in a house that should have settled down after a traumatic year, Mom and Dad and to a lesser extent the two girls, had more drama and trauma to follow.

Dorothy had her own room now. Shellee took over Marla's room when she moved out.

Dorothy who was still having nightmares no longer had a sister who would wake and come to her bed to comfort her. She had been in the clutches of that terrible man. She had smelled his breath and his body rot.

That's how her nightmares began every single time; with his smell. She woke with a start and her room was dark and empty the smell left her nightmare and settled like an old blanket, hovering over her.

Dorothy wrote about all this in her ledger. She no longer called it a diary because oldest sister Marla, when she gifted it, told Dorothy a diary should be place to capture wondrous thoughts and imaginings.

Dorothy was not thinking wondrous thoughts and imaginings but rather mean and nasty things she would have liked to do to that man. She called it her **Ledger; a place to keep count and keep track.**

Lying there drenched in sweat studying the darkened walls she suddenly sat up. She went to her desk and turned on her lamp. She opened her Ledger.

Her handwriting had changed from the loopy happy swirly multicolored writing of her earlier entries (pre- Aerial days) to a solid black printed form she barely recognized. This elementary child who had previously written of a good grade on a test, the gossiping she was privy to with a large circle of friends, the handsome new Social Studies teacher who was filling in for Miss Broden out on maternity leave, and her first dance ever, seemed to have disappeared.

Her pen hand seemed heavier now and bore down with more force. Her language changed and now contained swears when describing things whether at school or recreating her nightmares.

Tonight's nightmare had been particularly graphic. It seemed with each episode the action moved beyond the original trauma and became more explicit. Dorothy knew what sex was.

All kid nowadays seemed to be in the middle of one tryst or another no matter the time of day, the channel you turned to, or the social media platform you visited; whether treated as comedy or drama.

Tonight that terrible man, a man she now knew as Aerial Steward, didn't just threaten her and her sisters on the bus when he visited at night he shooed Marla and Shellee out the door and closed it behind them.

Dorothy in her dream watched her sisters disappear out the folding door of the bus and stand looking up pounding on the folded door trying to get back in. She couldn't hear them but she watched their mouths open and close and the tears stream down their faces.

Dorothy woke up in a cold sweat as accompanying the smells were his final words before he dismissed her sisters, 'I don't know who your father likes best but I choose you. He grabbed her as he closed the bus door' His eyes were soulless slits dead and distorted.

Standing alone Dorothy ran to the rear of the bus. Aerial Steward walked towards her a sick grin on his face. Tonight his hands seemed to reach through her nightmare. Dorothy knew for certain if those hands ever emerged from the darkness she would not survive.

Tonight when she woke covered in sweat she did something she had not done before; snapped on her lamp. It was if a fever had broken

A different more purposeful hand began putting pen to paper. This hand seemed to sift through different words and began to compose. Dorothy watched her hand move. This hand had found a root word; **EVIL.** This hand fumbled through her Thesaurus to find variations on the word **Evil.**

This hand spoke directly to the man by piling one word onto another. The writing appeared in a verse form.

I find you **PUTRID**, your **ROT** seems to linger.

I had never heard of **FETID,** but it sounds about right

LOW, VILE, STINKING, you give the world a finger.

The word **BLACK** doesn't work because before you appeared, I always loved the night.

Dorothy held her breath as this hand closed her ledger and turned off her lamp. She sighed deeply and went back to sleep with pictures in her head of labels containing the new words she was now armed with. For the rest of the night like a ninja throwing stars she attacked the man in her sleep.

All night long whenever Aerial Steward tried to enter her sleep she plastered the man from head to toe with yellow sticky notes. The man reeled under the onslaught and disappeared.

She awoke with an arsenal of ammunition to keep her nightmare at bay. She awoke rested for the first time in a long time.

The poem she composed became an anthem that played as each sticky note struck, high-lighting a descriptor.

This morning for first time in a very long time Dorothy came to the kitchen table with a smile on her face. She couldn't wait to use some of the words she had found. She couldn't wait to tell her family how she planned to manage her fears.

"Good morning team Garrett," she bubbled.

The three team members looked up and smiled wanly.

Wayne who had always been upfront with his family had just told daughter Shellee about his diagnosis of possible lung cancer. When he broke the news to Dorothy who had arrived late it deflated what she had wanted to finally reveal.

As a tearful hug and silent prayer rippled through Dorothy, a sudden thought struck her. *The same words she had penned last night that helped her sleep through the night might help her father if she applied them to this new invader.*

She started with the sentence, "You know Dad, **EVIL** can be beaten to a pulp." When she had everyone's attention she told them of all the anger she had been feeling over the last year.

Mom Becky folded her youngest daughter into her arms.

"But I'm ok Mom, I'm fighting back now."

Then she rushed to her room and returned with her ledger. She read them her poem. When she was finished, her mom with tears flowing encircled her youngest child once more.

Shellee too hugged her sister and said, "Seriously, poems and sticky notes."

Dorothy eyes wet but smiling answered, "Works for me."

Becky spoke, "Why didn't you tell us how you were feeling?"

"You and Dad had enough to worry about and I didn't want to be a baby."

Becky squeezed her daughter's shoulders."

"Anyway I'm not afraid anymore. He's dead and I'm covering his body with powerful words that will keep him dead. And Dad, these same words will work for you."

Wayne looked at his youngest daughter and tears filled his eyes. He nodded, no words necessary. He had raised strong young women.

Suddenly he stood. "I too will fight this new monster who has raised its ugly head."

He told them of Lying in bed this morning for a minute or two feeling sorry for myself. I have never smoked, what are the odds I asked myself. Why me?"

He reached out for hands that joined. "You guys have always thought of me as the strong one. That's not true."

Wayne squeezed the hands holding his and nodded his head. "It's all of us, its family strength." With that he rose and called for a group hug.

So a morning that had begun with revelations ended in one of resolve.

CHAPTER TWENTY-SIX

Marla and Crofton continued north. Marla upon being told of her father's health issues last evening was urged to continue her mission. "Don't cry for me Argentina," he kidded. "Jamie hasn't asked much of us over the years we need to help him find his grandson. I'll be fine."

Crofton was driving this morning as they made their way through very busy traffic on Interstate 95 well north of Jacksonville.

Florida as a state was changing its face at nearly every turn. New exits leading to new communities were being added to the spine of a roadway that stretched from Miami to Maine. Crofton fresh off the boat from Ireland was amazed by this country.

"Larger than a breadbox now isn't it?"

Marla looked across at him puzzled.

"All this." Crofton swept his arm from right to left taking in road construction that broadened the roadway and new exits being built in nearly every town or city they entered.

Marla nodded, "For sure Crofton and it's going to get larger. North is moving South."

"A lot of ground to cover to find one man. Do you suppose he wants to be found? Do you think he even knows he's lost?

"Let's hope."

The ride quieted as both receded into their own thoughts.

* * *

As fate would have it, like two ships in the night, "Jack the Ripper," traveling south, and Marla and Crofton driving north a mere fifty feet to his left, passed one another on Interstate 95.

* * *

When Jack reached Jacksonville he found the proper exit and left the highway. Following his mother's directions he maneuvered his way to the residential area where she was now living.

A well-manicured lawn greeted him as he turned into the driveway. He was facing a beautiful home that would summon half a million dollars or more in his estimation. *How times do change* he thought, remembering the dilapidated apartments he had lived in when he was a kid.

He took a deep breath and opened the car door. He wasn't even sure his mother would be glad to see him. He had not heard from her since a brief call for directions after sending a reply to her letter.

Palm trees framed the house and they seemed to be whispering, *don't expect much Jack, the dwelling may be different but she's your same old mother.* He knocked.

* * *

Marla and Crofton stopped in Brunswick, Georgia for an early lunch. They were comfortable with one another by now and kidding one another seemed to open nearly every conversation.

Crofton looked up at the menu board in the fast food restaurant they had agreed on. "Well Lassie" he grinned, "will you be having an Irish potato in some form to go with that sandwich you've chosen?"

Marla had to smile. "How do you stay so happy all the time?"

Crofton opened his mouth wide to reveal that set of extremely white teeth, "A good word never broke a tooth now did it?"

Marla simply shook her head and offered what she thought might pass for an Irish response, "I'll have a full grown fella still sporting his skin if it's available."

Crofton toasted her with his soft drink cup. "There's a kinsman in you Marla, I can feel it."

* * *

Jack's new step father answered the knock. He was big man with a florid complexion. *The man had obviously been a drinker in his time probably how the man met his mother,* thought Jack in the moment. Fake teeth gleaming pure white in a fake smile, *a dead giveaway in Jack's mind.*

The man's opening remarks cemented any doubt Jack might have had about how this was all going to go.

"Ripper is it?" A frown followed. "Your mother told me you might show up. She's not here but come on in for a minute." There seemed to be an emphasis placed on the word minute. He chuckled then, "I told her if you surfed in on a big wave while she was out I'd help you find the beach."

Jack had faced a lot bigger waves than the one standing in the doorway, so as if on the water waiting for a reason to stand on his board, he bided his time held his tongue and followed the man.

The house was large and sterile, nearly as white as the man's teeth. Jack was ushered into a formal living room that nearly blinded his eyes. White walls and drapes, off white sofa's, and paintings on the walls that proved money can't buy good taste.

When he had Ripper seated the man delivered what must have been an earlier agreed upon message.

"Your mother doesn't need to be bothered with all this. She sent that letter as a courtesy and only after I encouraged her to do so. "Did she tell you I used to be in law enforcement?"

Jack nodded.

"In my experience it's better to leave dead things dead and buried. Most times all you raise is a stink."

For a moment Jack sat stunned.

Then he rose, and never at a loss for words himself got in the last one before heading back to his car. He looked the man directly in the eye. "Being on the beach all the time I run across all kinds of dead smells. Seems stink can rise well away from the beach."

When the door closed behind him Jack was actually relieved. This mission was his own to navigate he didn't want his mother involved.

Jack found one of those beaches and spent the afternoon recharging his batteries by paddling hard into the ocean then rising to face whatever future might lie before him.

By the end of the afternoon Jack had made friends with a group of surfer dudes and secured a place to stay for the night. "not for a long time but for a good time," he promised.

CHAPTER TWENTY-SEVEN

Shellee Garrett was the middle child. Ever since her young sister Dorothy entered the picture a dozen years ago Shellee had become a dictionary's definition of **the middle child.** People say that's a real thing. The maxim held true for Shellee and unconsciously she adopted that role with no complaint.

In the Garrett household she wouldn't be the one holding the microphone during Karaoke she simply provided background harmony to any tune voiced. Often requests for her opinion on family matters were raised only as a tie breaker.

Shellee had thoughts though. She had fears and feelings too.

All during that terrible man's assault on her family she had mostly kept her thoughts, fears and feelings inside. She didn't find the words to battle her fears like her sister Dorothy she swallowed them.

Even at school Shellee seemed to be along for the ride.

But when her dad was diagnosed with lung cancer, those thoughts, fears, and feelings came roaring to the surface.

Older sister Marla was gone. Sister Dorothy had revealed her battle plans, now it was time for Shellee to allow her inner warrior to come out of the shadows.

Shellee spoke up and convinced her father to get a second opinion on his diagnosis. While she hadn't been the star of the show over the years she had always been an active listener.

That second opinion would change everything.

It was determined that Wayne Garrett didn't have lung cancer after all.

Stress it seems can attack the body in a hundred ways. In Wayne's case it mirrored a disease that thousands face.

Shellee was in the doctor's office with Wayne and Becky when the new results were announced.

"See I told you Dad." Shellee had earlier told her parents of her own health concerns during those turbulent times.

"I would wake up with what felt like a weight on my chest and could scarcely breathe. I honestly thought I was going to die."

"How did you know it was stress that was causing all that? You never said a word."

"My gym teacher who is also my soccer coach talked to the team about how a little stress is a good thing but too much stress over a longer time can make you sick."

"Okay I'm with you what else did he say?"

"We started out talking about throwing up before a game. Three or four of the kids said they did that. Anyway, I was feeling that weight on my chest all the time and after coach talked to us I did some research in the library."

"Shellee I don't think you've had this long a conversation with us in like forever, keep going."

"When I did the research I found that for people over fifty, long term stress can be really bad and can cause inflammation in the body that might actually kill you. I thought of you dad and the pressure of not being able to make things better when that man was trying to hurt our family. "

Becky took her daughter's hand.

"So I just thought you should get a second opinion."

Wayne took all this in on the ride home. It was obvious his girls were more resilient than he imagined.

* * *

So even as older sister Marla continued her quest to find Jamie Collins' grandson, back at the Garrett household good news arrived that promised their dad a bright new day

* * *

Ninety miles north in Jacksonville, "Jack the Ripper," woke up on a couch in an apartment that housed three young men who were attending <u>The University of North Florida.</u> Jack had met them the day before in the water. It wasn't long before he was giving surfing lessons to the trio.

Over beers that stretched well into the night war stories were swapped. Laughter trumped drama and the young men found a new friend in Jack.

Jack had never attempted to start college but the three took the mystery out of it and convinced him to visit the campus. "We will give you a tour, this place is the best kept secret in Florida," announced new friend, Arty.

So just two days in, "Jack the Ripper," was possibly raising his sights beyond finding a higher wave.

*   *   *

Three states north, Marla and Crofton were winding their way to an area called the Outer Banks of North Carolina. In her conversations with Flagler Beach Police Chief Dennis Cusack, North Carolina emerged as the state Aerial Steward had spent the most time since leaving Florida; on the water and often in hot water.

Crofton was driving and Marla was handling the map reading. They were still on 95 north and had Wilmington in their sights. They took the exit that put them on route 74 east. It was 3:35 pm. Crofton looked across the seat. "I'm hungry and tired what do you say we find a quiet little spot."

"I was thinking the same thing. It's too late to get to the beach and start asking questions anyway."

They continued their journey with Marla looking for a good place to eat. Crofton saw it first and gasped. "Isn't that a picture of Edgar Allen Poe on that sign?"

Marla simply said, "It says Poe's Tavern so I guess that's right. She kidded, do you know the man?"

"Marla the man is my literary hero. Let's stop and I will tell you all about it."

To refresh his memory, after being seated and ordering a sweet tea, Crofton excused himself to the little gift shop attached to the restaurant. He purchased a book of short stories along with Poe's most acclaimed poetry and brought it back to the table. He also brought back a map of the area and area businesses.

While Crofton stuck his nose in one of his purchases Marla looked at the map.

She studied the map and announced that it seemed they picked a good place to stop. She moved her finger along the map. Going forward with their mission they could bang a left onto West Salisbury Street or stay on 74 which would take them to one of the most famous surfing destinations on the East Coast.

When the waitress arrived with menus the two settled on the porch of Poe's Tavern and studied the offerings. Food with a Poe twist; Marla could not help chuckling. She was amazed that such a place existed and not the only one from what she was reading. "There are Poe locations in South Carolina, Georgia and Florida as well."

Crofton ordered the Black Cat Burger with grilled onions. Marla decided to try the Pit and Pendulum burger.

They ordered sweetened ice tea and were down to the cubes when a refill and their sandwiches arrived. Marla eyed Crofton's sandwich. "So tell me about the Black Cat."

Crofton pointed to the book he had just bought. "You really need to read it. It's a short story that hooked me completely the first time I read it. Remember I come from the land of the Folk Tale." Crofton took a sip of his sweetened tea. "Poe shared a lot of the characteristics we attribute to the Irish: He was an orphan, he was poor, he failed at many things, he died young, and was a probable alcohol and substance abuser." Crofton smiled. "Now if that's not a fair description of an Irishman I'll eat my hat."

Another sip then an end to the man's brief autobiography. "And like a good Irish folktale the man could really tell a story."

"So tell me a story Irishman."

"When I read <u>The Black Cat</u> I became a Poe lover. I think I've read nearly everything he wrote. Have you read any of his works?"

"In school we read <u>The Raven.</u> I think that's about it."

Crofton nodded even as he chewed.

"So tell me about this Black Cat you are devouring."

"Well in my school our teacher used Poe's poem <u>The Raven</u> to convince we boys that poetry wasn't a sissy sport. She was right. I love that poem. Anyway after that I looked up the man and found his story, <u>The Black Cat.</u>" Crofton opened the book and found the story.

As he scanned the pages the gist of the story reached his mind.

"Things start out innocently enough. This guy likes pets." Crofton left his narrative briefly.

"We all know cats can be unpredictable."

Marla whose family had no pets due to serious allergy issues, said "I'll take your word for it."

"Anyway one night the cat bites the guy." Crofton takes a bite of his burger and looks across at Marla who is keeping pace with her own burger. He chuckled to himself thinking, *I might just have to explain the story behind her menu choice, <u>The Pit And The Pendulum</u> burger.*

"So the guy gets bitten, what would we do? Maybe ban the cat to the shed, possibly even cuff him lightly."

A sip of tea fueled the story. "No, our guy punishes the cat by gouging out one of its eyes."

Marla's own eyes widened.

Crofton smiled. "But that horrible act doesn't seem to quell his anger. He hangs the cat from a tree." Crofton lets the story sit as he manages some fries. He continues to flip pages.

"There is a burning house in the story but I won't bore you with that. Anyway eventually another mostly black cat is procured only to once again raise the ire of the guy."

Marla speaks up, "Not a cat lover I take it, this Mr. Poe."

Crofton chuckled aloud and continued. "Did I tell you this man has a wife? Well he does."

A drumbeat of silence followed as Crofton let the story hang for a few seconds.

"His wife stops him from taking an ax to the cat."

Another bit of silence allows a swallow.

"Only to find she maybe should have left well enough alone."

Crofton with a twinkle in his eye moves on. "The man in the moment kills his wife instead of the cat." Crofton's eyes are smiling. He buries her in the basement behind a brick wall."

The police investigate the wife's disappearance and it looks like the man might get away with murder. But on a final check of the basement they hear a wailing cat who had accidently been walled in with the wife's body."

Marla had finished her burger and her fries.

"I can't say I wish I'd read that story but you told it well enough," chuckled Marla.

"I've just scratched the surface, let me tell you about the story you just ate."

Marla looked down at the lone French fry on her plate, daintily picked it up and waggled it in front of Crofton's face. "Maybe later right now we need to find a place to stay the night."

Crofton sat back and patted his filled belly as he looked around a tavern that was doing a robust business. *This can't be a one and done,* he thought. "Ok just promise me we get to eat here at least one more time before we leave town."

Marla wiped the catsup off her hand and offered her little finger. Crofton interlocked his own waiting for Marla to explain.

Marla looked him dead in the eye, "Pinky Swear."

Crofton scrunched his face in confusion. "Pinky Swear?"

Marla laughed, "It's a kid thing; a promise. Probably an old folk tale. I'm surprised you haven't heard it."

Crofton laughed out loud and spurted iced tea across the table.

With promises made the two adventurers left the tavern to find suitable lodging.

That night Crofton, sitting on the bed with his head against an enormous head board, told Marla more of what he knew of the famous poet and author, Edgar Alan Poe. Then he drew a comparison to the man who had set this mission on its course.

"That man who threatened your family he shared some commonality with old Edgar. Aerial Steward was a drunkard and while he didn't write horror stories he certainly put your family through one. He too died relatively young and who knows what mysteries lie ahead."

CHAPTER TWENTY-EIGHT

After a tour of the college, Jack made up his mind that someday he would return to this area. The three guys he met seemed to be forward looking with their lives and Jack knew it was time he did the same.

The guys seemed very normal and down to earth and didn't appear any smarter than Jack. *Maybe he could do college.* Jack once again entered 95 south. His cell rang. He pulled off an exit in St. Augustine and answered.

Jack's mother was on the line. "I apologize for my husband, he thought he was protecting me from my past. I'm sorry too for not answering the hundred questions you must have." She cleared her throat. Jack listened.

"I seem to recall something about Flagler Beach and your father possibly growing up in that area. Flagler Beach is pretty small maybe you could ask around."

"I appreciate it." An awkward silence filled the line, followed by a break in the call. Jack sighed. He decided since he had taken an exit to answer the call he would continue into St. Augustine and find a gas station that sold maps. *Where is Flagler Beach* he wondered, and *what is the best way to get there? And what will I find?*

On the outskirts of the city he stopped at a Race Track gasoline station. Jack didn't carry a credit card so he entered the store found a Florida map paid for thirty dollars' worth of gas, a cup of coffee and the map.

He filled his tank and then pulled to the side of the station to study the map. A million different thoughts entered his head as he sat there sipping. Jack took out the copy of his father's obituary. His father had died in Flagler Beach.

He found the city of Flagler Beach located on route A1A about thirty miles to his south and east. Second thoughts rose and he nearly turned back around. He had made some new friends in Jacksonville. Going forward seemed somehow a little scary. A series of questions entered his mind. *Where do I even start when I get there? What if I do find this man will he even remember my father?*

Jack's eyes followed route 1 on the map through St. Augustine to coastal A1A and then south towards Flagler Beach.

"I at least need to visit my father's grave if nothing else," he said aloud as he backed up shifted to drive and entered traffic.

Suddenly he had to compete with open busses carrying tourists to different parts of the city. He watched horse drawn carriages doing the same.

What a neat place this would be to spend some time, thought Ripper. After crossing the Bridge of Lions in St Augustine he reached route A1A and began his trip south.

CHAPTER TWENTY-NINE

Steve Hart, the deceased Aerial Steward's favorite plumber and part-time bartender at the <u>FISH OR CUT BAIT</u>, had some decisions to make. Within the past month his Uncle Steve passed away leaving Steve his house and several other properties. He also left his nephew a boatload of money.

Steve Hart was forty-five years old and now without the duties of caregiver spent his days going through his uncle's files and a houseful of stuff.

Steve continued to work part-time at the bar at night.

Steve visited his inheritance properties and determined he would need to do some serious rehab on the two duplex rentals. He also determined he would need to hire some manual labor to do that.

When he got to the bar he posted a message on the corkboard that held every kind of business card imaginable. Guys from all walks of life entered the bar and Steve decided it was the perfect place to conduct informal interviews for the help he needed.

Several thoughts crossed his mind in deciding to advertise in this manner. First, if someone took the time to read his message they must need work. Second, Steve would see the applicant at their possible worst.

* * *

"Jack the Ripper," spent his first night in Flagler Beach at a small family owned motel on the south side of the city. The next morning he went to the Flagler Beach Police Department.

He spoke to an officer at the desk. The officer went to his boss' office. Two minutes later Jack was entering the office of Police Chief Dennis Cusack.

The chief rose and shook Ripper's hand. "What's your name son?"

"You can call me Jack."

"Sit down and I'll tell you all I know about your father. I don't know much except his time in Flagler Beach was not positive."

Police Chief Cusack didn't sugar coat his story. By the time he finished, Jack sat there with his mouth agape.

Chief Cusack cleared his throat. "Would you like a cup of coffee or maybe some water?"

Jack shook his head still trying to take in all he had heard.

"I will say from what I have been told your father was having second thoughts about it all. Rumor has it he was planning to leave town the next day. He died before the sun rose. He told people he was going to try to find a lost son."

Jack couldn't believe what he was hearing.

"I recently spent a good deal of time with the family your father threatened. In particular the oldest daughter who is trying to find you as we speak."

"Why would she be doing that?"

"Apparently at the request of a possible relative of yours, a grandfather."

Jack took a deep breath. "What do you mean a Grandfather?"

Chief Cusack held up a hand. "That's the rumor. I don't know it to be true and I didn't know the man well. But what I do know of him was positive."

Chief Cusack wrote something on a piece of paper. "I can put you in touch with someone who has known him for years. His name is Wayne Garrett. It was his family that was threatened. Would you care to meet him?"

"I don't think I'm ready for that. If his number is on that paper I can call him after I get settled."

Jack left that meeting confused. Was there more to his father's message than just a man who had treated him kindly as a boy? Could he possibly have a grandfather? He returned to the motel and took stock of his possessions: an old beat up car, a surf board and just the clothes on his back.

If he was going to meet this possible grandfather he needed to have his act together. He needed to think, and he needed to be planning for a future; no better place than the beach.

He parked his old Subaru complete with a surf board securely attached, in one of the spaces that fronted the beach and entered the boardwalk. He had a towel from the motel and a bottled water in hand as he walked down to the water on a very different beach from what he was used to. Narrow, sloping, and very granular almost slushy. Didn't look like a beach you spent hours walking. But the waves looked inviting.

He watched as a handful of surfers paddled their way out, turn to face the beach, stand up and ride a sheet of water to the shallows.

What do I hope to accomplish? Now that he was here and might meet this possible grandfather he felt like he hadn't arrived with much of a work history. He had no education beyond high school, no job skills, no job; hell he was homeless. He chuckled to himself darkly, *would his grandfather think I'm just a clone of his son. A son he had never claimed apparently.*

The warmth of the day and the sounds of the surf overpowered him and he slept on a towel in the thick sand of Flagler Beach.

Toward evening he awoke and purchased a burger at Friends Café.

He wandered the downtown portion of A1A watching all the people. This was a very busy little city. As dark arrived he decided he wasn't ready to call it a day just yet. He found his way to a local tavern, the <u>FISH OR CUT BAIT</u>.

This is definitely a working man's bar, he thought to himself. A bulletin board just inside the doorway was pinned with a hundred business cards, lost pet posters, miscellaneous articles for sale, and available rentals. He scanned the list taking notice of several.

"Jack the Ripper" made his way to the bar. Not realizing it, he chose the very stool his father had very recently occupied.

Also not realizing it, he was about to be served by his father's favorite bar tender and plumber, Steve Hart

* * *

Police Chief Dennis Cusack had become good friends with Wayne Garrett and his family. After meeting Aerial's son he placed a call.

Wayne had finally received some positive news regarding his health. Was it the realization that the man who had spent the better part of a year threatening his family was dead? Was it the revelation his daughter Shellee provided regarding stress and your health? Was it the constant love his family had bestowed on him? Or maybe he was just getting physically stronger with therapy and becoming mobile once more? Whatever the reason, the shadows in his scans had disappeared.

When the phone rang Wayne was in the shower after a rigorous physical therapy session that he continued on his own at home. Wife Becky was harder on him than the crew that had worked him back to mobility. Wayne now envisioned his wife with a whip urging him to do just one more rep. He was kiddingly thinking about how he could use that whip during one of their love making sessions when he heard the phone ring.

Becky answered the phone. "Wayne's in the shower. How are you Chief on such an early morning?"

"I'm good actually. Haven't seen you guys for a while, let's catch up soon."

The line went quiet. The Chief cleared his throat, "Sorry for such an early call but I thought you should know, I had a visitor." He let that hang for a moment. "Aerial Steward's son has surfaced. At least he told me he was Aerial's son. He is going to give Wayne a call. He would like Wayne to put him in touch with Jamie Collins who I'm afraid I revealed might be his grandfather."

Becky was stunned. She stammered, "I don't know what to say. I'll have Wayne call you back."

"I know your daughter Marla is somewhere up north looking for the boy. I thought you ought to know. So yeah tell Wayne to call me. Talk with you soon."

Becky, after sharing this news with her husband, spent the day trying to reach her daughter Marla, but her calls went to voice mail.

* * *

After meeting with the police chief, Ripper had spent the day reflecting. Now looking at a myriad of bottles lining the back of a mirrored wall he spun on his stool. Sounds from a juke box in one corner drew his attention. The clack of balls striking one another on a pool table turned his head. A different wall was set up for darts. *The greasy smell of burgers and onions reached his nose. A working man's bar for sure.* Knowing his father had been a hard drinking man he wondered if he might have wandered into this very place in the past.

Bartender Steve watched the young man standing in the foyer. He spent some time looking at the bulletin board he seemed to study them. He also didn't seem in a hurry to down a drink. Steve watched him amble over to a stool and sit himself down and then begin a slow spin taking the place in. There was something familiar about him but Steve couldn't place him. *Had he served him before, hmm.*

A call for a beer sent Steve on a mission of mercy to a table in the rear.

* * *

Dwight Yoakum's song, <u>A Thousand Miles From Nowhere</u> filled the bar. Hanging like a cloud of smoke over conversation and at times influencing that conversation as stray lyrics were picked up and spit back out.

They seem to be having a good time, thought Ripper still spinning and unserved as yet.

"What can I get you young man, you are legal right?" Steve looked the young man in the eye.

Ripper who had been being served since he was sixteen, hauled out a very good likeness of himself with a legal birthdate and placed it on the bar.

Steve smiled. "Works for me." He continued to study the young man. "You remind me of someone I can't place just now. Been in here before?"

"Nope, new in town. What do you have for craft beers?"

"Hoppy or hazy, those are your two choices."

"I'm more of a hazy kind of guy, like a mid-summer day on the water if you know what I mean."

Steve nodded, "Hazy it is."

* * *

Up north, less than that thousand miles Dwight was singing about, another cliché was unfolding; <u>there was trouble in river city.</u>

That morning Marla dropped her phone. No big deal right? Well it's where it landed that was the problem. She had been crossing the street with coffee and bagels in hand when her phone rang.

As she crossed the center line trying to do three things at once, her phone still ringing left the two fingers fishing it out of her purse.

The street was just leaving darkness behind. Marla stopped, started, and tried to bend down while holding two cups of coffee and the bag of bagels. The phone ended up landing directly on the yellow line. She reached for it just as an engine roar reached her ears. Marla looked up into the jaw of a surfboard nearly covering the windshield of a small car. She dove to her right just as the bumper hit her in the shoulder.

The young woman stopped her vehicle and ran to hover over Marla who was now spread out as if she had toppled from that board into open water.

An ambulance arrived within minutes.

Marla Garrett was transported to <u>New Hanover Regional Medical Center</u>, in nearby Wilmington.

Crawford was in the shower while all this was happening. He toweled dry and turned on the television awaiting his coffee and a bagel. A half hour later he was still waiting.

Crawford didn't carry a cell phone though he was probably going to have to break down and get one now that he was in a relationship that might require a call now and then.

He dressed and walked towards the café Marla had gone to earlier. He passed an officer busy with a tape measure a short distance away. A cruiser with its blue lights still flashing seemed to be beckoning him but Crawford,

intent on finding Marla and his coffee, paid the scene no mind.

Marla was not in the coffee shop. Crawford, in the moment got a coffee to go and began to retrace his steps. Something wasn't right. He approached the officer.

"My girlfriend seems to be missing can you help?

CHAPTER THIRTY

Ripper decided to play his cards close to the vest and not share anything about his father with the bartender.

He nursed two beers and munched on a bowl of pretzels while listening to mostly country songs leaving the juke box. He could feel the eyes of the bartender meeting his whenever he glanced that way. The man seemed to be reaching way back in his skull trying to make a connection that eluded him.

When he left around 11pm. he stopped once more in the entrance and spent more time reading the message board. In his mind he didn't qualify for anything posted. In that moment of realization he decided he could not meet his grandfather under these conditions. He had work to do on himself first.

Bartender Steve was doing some thinking himself. For some reason he felt drawn to the young man who had remained mostly silent but observant, slowly spinning on a particular stool. A stool that Steve would forever identify as Aerial Steward's. He watched the young man pause in the entry and again study the board. Was he looking for work? If he came in again Steve just might offer up a good old manual labor opportunity.

* * *

Crofton arrived at the hospital just as Marla was being taken to a room. After identifying himself as Marla's fiancée he was ushered to a waiting room. He was promised her doctor would be in after reading the results of the tests. Crofton was told Marla was awake and coherent.

An hour later the doctor entered the waiting room and told Crofton the good news. Marla was banged up but would eventually be as good as new. "Her shoulder is broken but all in all she was a very lucky young woman. She was told you were here and wants to see you."

Crofton nodded, "God's help is nearer than the door."

The doctor appeared stymied.

"I could have said it's the luck of the Irish that saved her but even an Irishman knows when to defer to a higher power."

"I think you might just be right about that. I'll walk you in."

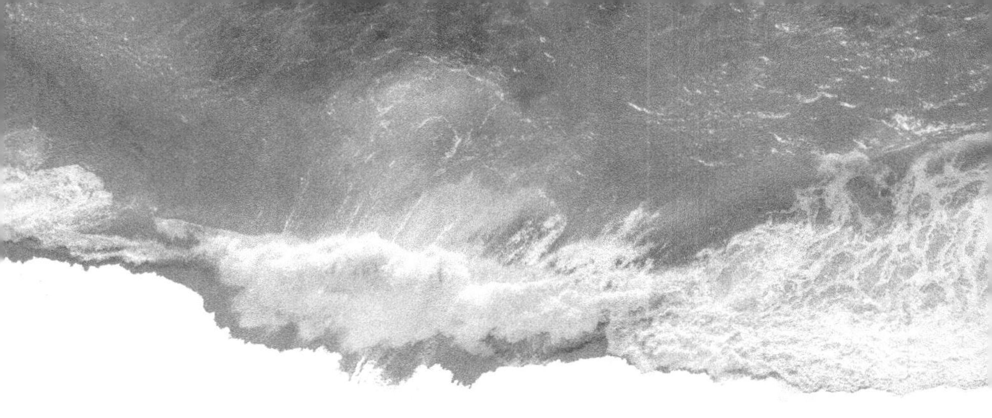

CHAPTER THIRTY-ONE

Most of us don't choose when we are to die. For Jamie Collins it could not have come at a more inopportune time. But in the truest spirit of an Irishman trying to maintain control until the very end Jamie, put a plan into motion.

Just as poor Marla was dodging her own demise in the middle of that road in North Carolina, Jamie Collins was taking his last breath.

He had prepared for this day knowing he wanted to have the last word on the subject of Jamie Collins.

A carefully penned letter set unread in his room. It was to be placed in the trust of Wayne Garret. The same Wayne Garrett was to scatter his ashes and his wishes in the directions Jamie intended.

When Wayne arrived to make arrangements for the body, he found the letter. He took a seat in Jamie's recliner and began reading.

> **Dear Wayne, if you are reading this then my pen's trace remains while the hand that held it dies.**

Words are more lasting than the wealth of the world. I have been honored to be your lifelong friend. You created a strong family from pixie dust and tended a garden of love that will flourish for ever more.

My own life has been as a watcher. I never could seem to find the formula necessary to create a family of my own.

In the end it seems I might have actually been a father and grandfather, way too late to enjoy the moments and the memories.

Please find my last will and testament and take proper care of a possible grandson who I had yet to meet.

In closing I will loosely paraphrase the late Oscar Wilde for he seems to have been thinking of me when he penned the following words:

Misfortunes one can endure—they come from outside, they are accidents. But to suffer for one's own faults—Ah! There is the sting of life.

So Wayne my time is up. I will end this talk simply by closing my mouth.

Uncle Jamie

* * *

Two calls had come into the Garrett home within minutes of one another. The first came from Marla's new friend, Crofton.

Daughter Shellee answered the phone. Becky and Wayne were out food shopping on this midmorning.

"This is Crofton your sister's friend. Let me start by saying your sister is fine but she has been in an accident."

Shellee didn't panic at the word accident, she simply took a deep breath. "Go on."

Crofton told the story in an understated way trying not to frighten Marla's sister.

"Let me give you the number for the hospital to pass along to your parents. Please let them know Marla is going to be okay."

The phone hadn't even had the opportunity to absorb Crofton's call before it rang once again.

This time it was the retirement home calling for Wayne. Shellee told them her dad wasn't home. "Please ask your father to call the retirement home at his earliest."

Shellee promised she would get in touch with her father immediately, and then hung up. Deep breaths resumed even as she dialed.

* * *

Ripper sat at a picnic table nursing a cup of coffee locking out over the Atlantic Ocean. From his vantage point he could see the outside seating filling up at a local restaurant, <u>The Funky</u> <u>Pelican</u>. He was close enough to hear the laughter and see what looked to be family and friends gathering to enjoy good food and one another. He became a little reflective in the moment. He turned his head and watched a single surfer paddling his way out to deep water. *That is me* he thought. He turned his head back to the restaurant. He could not recall ever being part of a family going out to breakfast.

He fingered the slip of paper that Police Chief Cusack had given him. Was that number going to change his life? Was he going to be part of someone's family?

What had been a light cloud cover slowly dissipated and the sun emerged warming his body and thoughts. He took a sip of cooling coffee.

He nodded and spoke aloud. "It's on me. I have to make what I want to happen, happen." He emptied the cold coffee into the soil, crumpled the cup and left the beach to clean up. He had a destination. Job one on this new day was to revisit the message board at the watering hole, <u>FISH OR CUT BAIT</u>.

CHAPTER THIRTY-TWO

Life can be viewed as a series of connections. For the Garrett family, a year that began with a simple act of delivering the mail, was not done delivering surprises.

Wayne and Becky hurried home. Their shopping cart of groceries left in aisle 8. Shellee had not given them the particulars she just told them to come home immediately. Her voice betrayed the urgency however.

During the fifteen minute ride Wayne and Becky imagined all kinds of drama. Becky was driving. Wayne placed his hand on her knee gathering strength from her warmth.

"Wayne there's no sense in worrying or speculating, we've weathered the very worst in the last year. We will weather whatever is waiting at home."

Shellee and her sister were sitting on the front steps. Seeing the two girls apparently safe and sound allowed Wayne to eliminate some of his stress.

Becky took his hand and they walked calmly to the porch and sat down one on either side of the two girls.

Shellee took a breath. "Two things, first off Marla was in an accident but she's going to be okay. Crofton called. He left a number for the hospital." She let that sit to be absorbed. Becky took Dorothy's hand. Wayne reached for Shellee's.

"I think Jamie Collins has passed away. The retirement home called. They wouldn'tme he died but I'm sure he did."

Oddly Wayne had not considered either possibility when his mind had raced the speed limit home.

Becky went into the house and returned with the number for the hospital. Even in moments of distress, Becky's mind remained playful. "I'll call and check on Marla first, Uncle Jamie is apparently not going anywhere, or he's already somewhere." The girls shifted seats so that their parents were now seated side by side hands touching.

Wayne didn't speak but chuckled aloud at his wife's logic and sense of humor.

Shellee thought this was a good time to leave her parents alone with their thoughts so corralled Dorothy to go in and make some comfort food; Blueberry pancakes.

The hospital connected Becky with her daughter's room and Marla answered on the first ring. When she heard her mother's voice Marla broke down for the first time.

When she had gathered herself she told her mom the whole story. She would be dismissed later in the day and she and Crofton would spend the night on the road and then come home.

Becky shared the news of Jamie's death. More crying traveled a thousand miles of air space with both women blubbering.

Becky handed the phone to Wayne.

The call ended with Marla assuring her dad she would check in tonight.

After a breakfast of pancakes and hugs all around Wayne backed out of his driveway. Suddenly he stopped. Looking him dead in the eye was his mailbox. His mind immediately filled with the hundreds of messages that box had delivered over the years. No judgements, no emotions, just a messenger for useless flyers or information or in some cases messages of hope; in the last year, messages of meanness and hurt. Wayne had spent his whole career believing in the postal system. Staring at his mailbox now confirmed his belief. *Don't shoot the messenger.* He set his face to neutral and headed to the retirement home.

* * *

Ripper was squeaky clean, all dressed up in a new blue denim long sleeved shirt with all its buttons and a new pair of khaki cargo pants. On his feet he wore bright green Crocs. He found himself whistling as he walked to the bar. It was just past two pm when he entered. He studied the board once again. The message that struck him with the most possibilities was the one with the heading, "Jack of all trades master of none."

Check with the bartender if sober and interested the message continued.

Hell I'm a Jack at least, he thought. And I'm sober.

The bartender he would need to talk to was not on duty. The man he would be talking to was named Steve and he'd be in around five.

He must be the guy I met last night that was giving me the stink eye, thought Ripper.

"I'll be back," offered Ripper.

* * *

Wayne had spent the mid-morning gathering together all Uncle Jamie's effects. He found the letter and spent some time in quiet reflection while sitting in Jamie's recliner. The bed had been stripped bare and Jamie was now resting comfortably in a funeral home in Palm Coast.

Wayne called Jamie's lawyer and set up a meeting. There was to be a funeral which was yet to be planned. Wayne called home to Becky and asked her to call the funeral home and make arrangements.

"I'll be home in a while I need a little alone time to absorb all this. Think I'll take a walk, maybe on the beach. I love you honey."

So Wayne drove to the beach and walked the route he used to take when returning from his paper route. All he had learned about Ariel Steward came back to mind by the time he reached the boardwalk on Flagler beach. His mind returned to the time Aerial asked him to give up his new paper route. What a strange series of events had transpired from a single meeting all those years ago.

And poor Uncle Jamie, deprived of the knowledge that he indeed had a son until much too late to be a father and then even more recently the knowledge of a grandson. May he rest in peace.

Wayne reread the letter.

With Marla coming back home to heal it seemed it would be up to Wayne to fulfill Uncle Jamie's last wishes.

Just as days ago Marla had been within fifty yards of Aerial's son while traveling in two different directions, Wayne was soon to be in even closer proximity to Jamie Collins' grandson, Ripper.

Steve Hart spent the morning and afternoon tearing out a wall in one of his newly acquired tenement buildings. Black mold had invaded one of the walls and Steve was seeking its source. When he removed the sheet rock he immediately found a stain that seemed to be coming from the attic. After climbing the narrow steps to an abbreviated space that merely hid the truss system, he visually traced a water stain that followed a horizontal truss right to its point of entry. He approximated where on the roof the water was coming from and left the attic. He climbed a ladder and found several damaged shingles on the roof.

Steve left that afternoon more determined than ever to find a healthy young man who would be willing to do the grunt work required to correct all this.

He entered the bar at 4:45pm and looked at the message board, his job listing was missing.

He clocked in and entered the bar area and dawned the leather vest that identified him as an employee.

Steve checked his watch. He gazed out over a small group of mostly empty tables. It would be an hour or more before the place started hopping. Three stools were occupied. A couple of regulars and a man Steve didn't recognize. The man looked out of place. He wandered down the bar to the newbie.

"Welcome to <u>FISH OR CUT BAIT</u>, I see you are drinking a bud light, can I buy you the next round?"

Wayne glanced up seemingly confused. He chuckled aloud. "I haven't been in a bar for ages, things have surely changed if bartenders are now paying for the drinks."

Steve smiled, "I guess I'm not your typical bartender. I noticed you seemed lost in your glass, a lot on your mind?"

Wayne sighed. He had four women on his mind, a funeral to plan for, and Jamie's missing grandson to find. "You could say that and you would be right." He looked at his mostly empty glass then held it up. "Sure if you're buying I would like a drink that honors an old friend who recently passed."

"Whatever you want, just don't get too complicated."

"How about a Jameson Whiskey dressed for the winter months in a sweater of Baily's Irish Cream?"

Steve laughed aloud. "Never heard it described that way before."

"My friend was a true Irishman and nothing he ever uttered was expressed without humor, or extreme gravity, or an Irish witticism attached."

Upon delivery of the drink a conversation ensued. Whiskey loosens the tongue and before the clock clanged 7:00, between Steve filling drink orders, the two men exchanged life stories.

Steve told Wayne he had in fact met Aerial Steward both here at the bar and at Aerial's trailer where he mended his pipes. He expressed empathy for what the man had put Wayne's family through. "He was in here sitting right where you are now the night he died."

Wayne took a long sip of Jameson's. "Now I'm charged with trying to find the man's son, a promise made to my recently expired friend."

Wayne finished what had turned into (metaphorically speaking) a very cold night. Poor Jameson had worn three sweaters by the time Wayne dragged himself from the stool to begin a tipsy walk to his home. "I left my car a ways up the beach so I'll be walking home. He shook off Bartender Steve's suggestion of getting a cab. "I'll be walking my way to sobriety as my late and great friend Jamie Collins would say."

Just as Wayne reached that wall of messages, the outer door opened. Passing within a foot of one another, a teetering Wayne Garrett and a young and eager Ripper Steward exchanged glances and polite nods.

Remembering the days his own father coming home drunk when Ripper was barely five, an immediate thought reached Ripper's mind. *I hope this guy's kids don't have to put up with what I had to.*

Ripper entered and slung himself onto a particular bar stool. The seat was warm. The bartender from the other night was not visible. Ripper took two pieces of paper from his pocket and smoothed them out placing them on the bar.

Steve came from the small kitchen area carrying a burger and fries and proceeded to a table in the back. He casually noticed the young man who had been here yesterday occupying the same bar stool. Once more Steve was struck by an unconscious recognition. Once back behind the bar he approached Ripper Steward.

"Are you still lost in the haze or would you like something different tonight?"

"I'll make another run with that hazy brew, thank you very much." He folded the number that would put him in touch with Wayne Garrett, then pointed to the paper message remaining. "Are you the man hiring?"

Steve flopped a bar towel over his shoulder. "I am. Are you interested?"

Ripper nodded. "Ready willing and able, that's me."

Steve chuckled to himself. He had actually decided to approach the young man with an offer of employment if he ever returned. He stuck out his hand and reintroduced himself.

Ripper started to respond but then hesitated. He pointed at the message heading. "I'm Jack. Jack as in a **Jack of all trades** I guess. The two men shook hands.

Ripper didn't stay long. His new boss said they would be on a roof at first light.

Ripper left feeling better about himself than he had in a long time. He fingered the phone number in his pocket. If this gig worked out he might be meeting his grandfather with at least a few dollars in his pocket and fully employed.

CHAPTER THIRTY-THREE

Time passed. Wayne Garrett was back to work full time while Becky decided she needed a change and was in the process of getting her Realestate license.

When Wayne inherited several of Uncle Jamie's properties, Becky began managing the renters. She got very interested in the dos and don'ts and decided she needed to know more about buying and selling and renting and leasing.

Oldest daughter Marla was home, healed and still attached to Crofton. They were both enrolled at Flagler College in St. Augustine, Florida and sharing an apartment off campus.

Becky had negotiated their first rental and saved them a hundred a month.

Dorothy had become a serious young woman in middle school. She developed a flare for writing which had gotten its start during what, Oldest sister Marla, had dubbed our, **Bleak House** year; having read the Charles Dicken's novel of that name.

Shellee Garrett was turning sixteen today. She was now the family risk taker having decided life was too short to let fears drive your actions.

She had taken up surfing with a vengeance. Nearly every morning she took at least one ride on the waves before driving herself to school fresh off getting a license.

She was usually alone during those morning hours, but when school dismissed in the afternoon she gathered with a group of like-minded friends and rode till the sun went down.

On one of those late afternoons she noticed a very talented surfer who seemed to defy gravity on the water. She didn't know his real name. One of her friends thought it was "**Riptide**" or something like that.

* * *

Ripper had become a god send for Steve. The young man was on time, focused, clean and sober and a good conversationalist to boot.

During the past six months the young man had truly become the master of everything Steve challenged him with.

One afternoon about three months into their working relationship they finished the complete overhaul of the building with the leaky roof and black mold motif.

"I'm putting this on the rental market tomorrow. If you are tired of my spare room I'll rent it to you as cheaply as I can."

Jack bobbled his head as he thought. A month ago he shared his story with Steve. Steve convinced him he should call this Wayne Garrett and find out if his grandfather was still alive.

Jack let more time pass..

When Wayne and Jack finally met officially for the first time they eyed each other curiously. A smile crossed Jack's face. *I bet he doesn't even remember me in that entry-way standing there three sheets to the wind* thought Jack. *Well I won't remind him.*

That first formal meeting took place at a family barbecue celebrating Shellee's birthday. When first introduced as Aerial's son things became a little bit solemn in the moment. Jack sat back saying nothing, what was there to say? Shellee recognized the surfer she saw on the water and was the first to engage. With the ice broken (just as Crofton with his charm and wit had won the family over) Jack soon had the entire family laughing.

Wayne in turn shared some Uncle Jamie stories he had never told the family, stories that let Jack know what a kind and benevolent man his grandfather was.

After dinner Wayne brought out a copy of Jamie's will and told young Jack he had been named in the will and a significant amount of money would be waiting for him on his twenty first birthday.

"He wanted you to know he loved you even if you had never met. If there is anything we can ever do for you please ask."

Jack the Ripper nodded his head. He let his eyes reach each member of the family. "I apologize for all my father put your family through. I never really knew him. He left when I was young. I do remember he never hugged or kissed me. He always smelled of liquor and stale breath. My mother wouldn't talk about him."

"Well we survived as a family and I think we're even stronger than before," said Becky.

"Let's cut the cake," said Dorothy changing the subject.

While Shellee stood looking at the lighted cake she was told to make a wish. She didn't hesitate.

Today was the first time she had met Jack in person. He was taller and better looking up close. She held her breath then blew out the sixteen candles with a flourish. Younger sister Dorothy asked what Shellee wished for.

Shellee looked directly at Jack. "I'm glad to meet you in person Jack and to know your name isn't **Riptide.**" The family laughed. "I do have a wish that is really a request. Will you help me become a better surfer?"

Jack was slack jawed. He looked at Wayne and Becky as if seeking permission to speak. Both parents met his eyes and nodded.

"I would be glad to give you lessons. If there is one thing I am actually good at it's riding a board."

CHAPTER THIRTY-FOUR

Marla and Crofton were both studying for a business degree at Flagler College. They decided they would like to own a business together. They even had an idea what that business would be. Crofton did the research.

The original Poe's Tavern had opened on Sullivan's Island in South Carolina in 2003. Poe had been stationed there when he was in the army.

Crofton and Marla on their way to Wrightsville Beach to find Aerial Steward's son had discovered Poe's Tavern. They both fell in love with the place. Crofton had Marla reading Poe's poems and narratives and the whole idea of maybe opening a restaurant blossomed when they became enamored with the city of St. Augustine. The only Poe's tavern in Florida was on Atlantic Beach in Jacksonville Florida.

St. Augustine seemed like it would be a natural fit.

Marla as well as her two younger sisters had inherited a healthy chunk of change from Uncle Jamie. Crofton's family had money.

The two just needed to get up to speed on the business side of things. "Hell the menu is set and the business model is unique, it will be a destination place. St Augustine is a destination place. We will do well here."

So with three years to go to secure their bachelor degrees at Flagler College, they began to research just what they needed to do to become a franchise owner.

* * *

Youngest daughter Dorothy continued to use her ledger to keep track of her family and her own experiences. When she was given an English assignment to write how she channeled her feelings, her written response blew her teacher away.

"You have created a whole new way to use words. Do you have more examples written down? If you do I think you should publish a book."

So at the ripe old age of thirteen, Dorothy Garrett became a published author.

* * *

Jack and Shellee rode surfboards right into a relationship. When the two discovered they had feelings for one another, Jack twenty, asked Wayne and Becky how they would feel about he and Shellee dating.

"We have never seen Shellee so happy. Just treat her well, you have our blessing."

The End.

{Not}

AFTERWARD

When this story began we followed three sisters down the stairs to what was to be an ongoing drama. We were looking at a family in crisis. Threatened from an unknown source, their daily life forever changed.

When we looked back six months we saw a very different family.

We were introduced to a happy man who loved his family and his job. He was content to spend his evenings walking the beach with wife Becky, daughters Marla, Shellee, and Dorothy.

The normalcy of the Garrett family was rudely interrupted by a troubled soul.

A year of pain and suffering, both physically and emotionally, followed. You know that to be true, as a reader, you witnessed it.

As the band Rascal Flats told us in the song playing the night Aerial Steward passed from this earth; **The family moved on.**

Now let's catch up with the family three years later and bring this story full circle.

* * *

The stairs still groan with every step taken. The railing squeaks as hands seek purchase. The kitchen, the morning focal point, is alive as still to this day everyone is normally responsible for securing their own breakfast.

But not this morning.

This is a special morning. Dorothy Louise Garrett graduates today. She is a published author of poetry and shortly after receiving her diploma will begin a position with a nationally recognized magazine.

Marla and Crofton arrived late last night and are the last to navigate the stairs. They recently opened a **Poe's Tavern** in St Augustine. They also recently became engaged.

Shellee, and new husband, Jack the Ripper, were the first up and down the stairs. They have already spent an hour on the water. Shellee is working for a non-profit company that addresses climate concerns in a myriad of ways.

Jack the Ripper, Jack of all trades and master of none, is now working for his mother-in-law Becky. He has claimed the inheritance left by his grandfather Jamie and he and Shellee live in the bottom apartment of the four story tenement just as his grandfather did years ago.

As for Steve Hart, he was recently called back to the frozen north and has sold the three apartment buildings and the house he inherited from his uncle to the <u>Becky Garrett Real Estate Company.</u>

Wayne is busy whipping up pancakes and Becky is serving coffee to the ever widening group surrounding the kitchen table.

Wayne looks out the kitchen window while the pancakes cook. His eyes are drawn to the mailbox. He sighs inwardly. He looks around the table and nods to the blessings he has received. He watches his wife circling the table with a coffee pot. He smiles, their eyes meet.

Tonight, thinks Wayne who after all is a just a simple man, tonight before he sleeps he will get to enjoy all that makes Becky so special. (That whip never made it past his imagination.)

Wayne looks out the window once more. The mail truck is stopping up and down the street.

Wayne has taken early retirement from the post office and helps Jack maintain their properties.

Wayne inherited a sizable amount of money and property from Uncle Jamie that allows both Becky and himself to enjoy life at a more leisurely pace.

Wayne looks out the window once more. The mail truck is stopping at his box. An arm emerges from the vehicle's window. Wayne is suddenly struck by a motto he followed for years.

While there is no official motto for the postal service it is clear that no matter the version you have heard its meaning is clear;

Through hell or high water, THE MAIL MUST GO THROUGH!

www.ingramcontent.com/pod-product-compliance
Lightning Source LLC
Chambersburg PA
CBHW070341200726
48294CB00003B/748